"I think you need to put that baby in protective custody," Austin said.

He glanced away, then back at her. "So you can do your job and get beyond this threat."

Kylie couldn't believe what she was hearing. "So I can do my job?" Was that what mattered the most to him?

Austin stepped toward them, his hand gestures [illegible] indicating he was [illegible] died out there."

"I know that. Don't [illegible] anything she want[illegible] thought of being separated from the baby nearly broke her in half.

Austin was right, though—something bad could have happened to Mercedes.

It was clear he was uncomfortable with her new status as a single mother. He just wanted her to be Kylie: unattached, trusted border patrol agent.

He would have to accept she was a package deal now.

* * *

Texas Ranger Holidays: A Season of Danger

Thanksgiving Protector by Sharon Dunn
Christmas Double Cross by Jodie Bailey
Texas Christmas Defender by Elizabeth Goddard

Ever since she found the Nancy Drew books with the pink covers in her country school library, **Sharon Dunn** has loved mystery and suspense. Most of her books take place in Montana, where she lives with three nearly grown children and a spastic border collie. When she isn't writing, she enjoys hiking with her husband enjoying God's beauty.

Books by Sharon Dunn

Love Inspired Suspense

Texas Ranger Holidays

Thanksgiving Protector

Witness Protection

Top Secret Identity

Texas K-9 Unit

Guard Duty

Dead Ringer
Night Prey
Her Guardian
Broken Trust
Zero Visibility
Montana Standoff
Wilderness Target
Cold Case Justice
Mistaken Target
Fatal Vendetta
Big Sky Showdown

THANKSGIVING PROTECTOR

SHARON DUNN

HARLEQUIN® LOVE INSPIRED® SUSPENSE

Special thanks and acknowledgment to Sharon Dunn for her participation in the Texas Ranger Holidays miniseries.

Recycling programs for this product may not exist in your area.

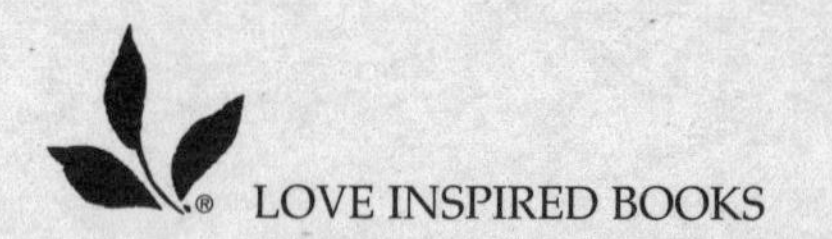

ISBN-13: 978-0-373-45736-6

Thanksgiving Protector

This edition published by arrangement with Love Inspired Books.

www.Harlequin.com

Printed in U.S.A.

Give thanks to the Lord,
for He is good and His love endures forever.
—*Psalms* 106:1

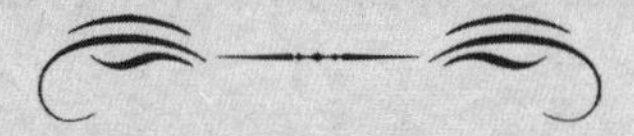

This book is dedicated to my Aunt Kathy and Uncle Bill for taking me in all those years ago and being Jesus with skin on. I will always be thankful for your love and wisdom and my life will never be the same because you opened your hearts to me.

ONE

Bad things happen at night.

Border patrol agent Kylie Perry stared through her night vision goggles and repeated the words that had kept her alive every time she went out on patrol at this hour—words that reminded her to be prepared for anything.

Tonight could be big. All intel pointed to the drug lord Rio Garcia crossing the border into El Paso from Juarez, Mexico. Rumor had it he was coming to seek revenge on his sister, Adriana, who had betrayed him.

Catching Garcia would be a coup for both the border patrol and the Texas Rangers she was working with tonight.

With the rushing rumble of the Rio Grande current pressing on her ears, Kylie scanned the high thin grass that surrounded the river.

A voice burst through the radio. "I've got movement at ten o'clock." Austin Rivers, one of the rangers she was assisting, couldn't hide his excitement. Apparently, he liked the action as much as she did.

Kylie's heart skipped into double time as she turned her head toward where Austin had indicated. She scanned until her view took in one person moving at a rapid pace across the river. That couldn't be their target. Rio Garcia would have four or five henchmen with him. He never went anywhere without his bodyguards.

But maybe he was changing tactics.

"Kylie, let's see if we can catch him." Austin's voice came through the radio. "The rest of you hold your position. This could be nothing."

Heart racing, adrenaline surging. Kylie took off running. A moment later, she heard Austin's footsteps behind her. Her feet pounded the ground. She knew the fastest route to the river. Because of their knowledge of the people, terrain and geography, border patrol was an invaluable asset on these ranger missions.

The glowing figure disappeared in the tall brush on the American side. One person alone. Who could it be? She couldn't tell if the yellow glow she'd seen through the night vision goggles had been a man or woman.

Kylie quickened her pace as she gulped in air.

As they approached the river, she slowed down and drew her weapon. Austin came up beside her and pulled his gun, as well. She scanned the landscape looking for the solitary figure. Her ears tuned into every sound. Austin pressed close to her, their shoulders nearly touching.

Minutes passed as the tension bore down on her and twisted her stomach in a knot. The high-wire tension was made worse by the sweat that trickled down Kylie's neck. Even a November night in this area felt hot to her. She was a Montana girl, born and bred. As much as she loved her job, she wasn't sure she would ever get used to the desert climate of El Paso.

Austin whispered as he pivoted and aimed his gun at each sector of the landscape. "Are you sure your informant was right about Garcia coming over tonight in this spot?"

"All my information from her so far has been golden," Kylie said.

Most informants were criminals themselves, men and women on the take wanting money or criminal charges against them dropped. This one was different. Kylie had met Valentina and her six-month-old baby, Mercedes, at her church. When Valentina found out Kylie was a border agent, the young mom had offered Kylie a deal. Valentina would pass vital information to her in exchange for prepaid classes at a community college. Kylie's boss had readily agreed to the arrangement.

Kylie admired that Valentina wanted to make a better life for herself and her baby.

The sound of her own breathing surrounded Kylie as fear mingled with anticipation. The goggles turned the bushes and desert an eerie shade of green. It was the iridescent glow of a human on the move that Kylie searched for.

A tension wove through the silence.

"Did we lose him?"

What sounded like fireworks on the US side erupted not far from them. Kylie thought she saw flashes that could be gunfire off to the east. Her heartbeat revved up. Every muscle tensed, ready for action.

This was it.

"Maybe that's the planned distraction your informant told you about." Austin ran toward the noise. Kylie sprinted to catch up to him.

According to Valentina, Garcia's plan was to create a diversion at one of the checkpoints so he and his henchmen could slip unnoticed across this unmarked area.

Maybe Garcia had switched up the locations or maybe Garcia had run into trouble from a rival cartel. In any case, they needed to check it out.

Austin spoke into his radio. "All rangers. Fall in. Sounds like a gunfight out there."

Kylie pushed through the brush in the direction of the disruption. She hurried up a trail littered with garbage bags, dirty diapers and hypodermic needles. This was the path the illegals took once they made it across the river, the debris a testament to the danger of their struggle.

Because she knew the area better, Kylie took the lead as they sprinted across the desert. By the time the ground leveled out, both of them were out of breath. Still, they rushed into the darkness toward the danger. Her goggles picked up nothing human, no yellow glowing figures.

Several more shots were fired. She flinched at each shot but kept running.

As if on cue, both of them ducked down into the sagebrush.

The quiet settled in as they eased forward toward where the ruckus had taken place.

Her heart racing, Kylie continued to scan for movement. Then she saw it—a body lying on the ground completely still. She edged in closer and flipped up her goggles. She was near enough now to see details illuminated by moonlight. It was a woman, and a familiar tattoo on her forearm caught Kylie's eye.

Dread gripped her throat. "I'm going in to identify."

"Kylie, no. The area is still hot."

Austin's words echoed in her head. He was right. Yet, she felt compelled to run toward the lifeless body.

Her feet pounded the hard desert earth. Ignoring protocol, she shone a light on the dead woman lying facedown. She took in the long dark hair, the familiar rose tattoo on the right arm. Gently, she turned over the body. Her heart squeezed tight and all the air left her lungs.

"Valentina." Her voice filled with anguish.

She felt herself go numb inside as her knees buckled. In an instant, Austin was beside her, gripping her arm, holding her up.

Kylie shone the light on her friend's face. The letter *T*, drawn in black marker on her forehead, stained the sweet woman's lifeless features.

"Kylie, we need to take cover now." Austin's voice seemed to come from a million miles away.

More gunfire filled the night as Kylie felt herself drowning in pain and confusion. Only Austin's hand clasping her forearm kept her from falling apart as he dragged her out of the line of fire.

Adrenaline flooded Austin's body as he pulled Kylie toward the protection of the tall brush. High-pitched rifle shots from a distance pierced the night. Snipers from the Mexican side. Cartels always hired them to take out law enforcement when they were crossing. Rio Garcia had his fingerprints all over this one.

Austin didn't know who the fallen woman was, but the death had clearly affected Kylie enough to shake her. More gunfire cut through the night. Judging from the sound, it was a pistol being fired at close range on the American side of the border. It looked like whoever had shot the dead woman was now targeting Kylie and him. Austin's gaze darted around. What was taking the rest of the ranger team so long?

They ducked behind some high bushes. At least one henchman and maybe Garcia were out there in the darkness.

The other rangers must be on their way.

Austin spoke into his radio. “Requesting air support. Agent Perry and I are under heavy fire. Some at close range. We have a dead civilian female.”

“Her…her name was Valentina.” Kylie’s voice cracked.

Kylie knew the dead woman. No wonder she’d fallen apart. That *T* on the forehead meant *traidor*, Spanish for *traitor*. Maybe this was the informant Kylie had placed so much confidence in.

Another shot whizzed by so close it left his ears ringing. Kylie fell to the ground after him. Her reactions were off, too slow.

Still listening for shots or other activity around them, he sat up, turned to face her and gripped her shoulder. “Kylie, we’ve got to get these guys. Are you with me… for your friend?”

She nodded, pulled herself up and clicked her goggles back into place.

Maybe she hadn’t recovered from the shock of seeing Valentina dead, but Kylie was so well trained that she could go on autopilot if she had to. The truth was he’d requested working with Kylie for the Garcia mission for three reasons.

First, she was professional. Second, she could be trusted. And third…something about her smile and easy laughter made him look forward to going to work that much more. He and Kylie would never be more than colleagues. He’d written off the possibility of a wife and kids long ago. He could better serve his God and people by being a ranger without attachments. But he could enjoy her company without getting in over his head, couldn’t he?

He waited until he heard the whir of the Black Hawk blades before moving through the brush in the direction of the gunfire. Only one more shot was fired before the helicopter came into view. Now they had the shooter or shooters on the run.

A border patrol agent in the chopper used a spotlight to light up the desert and hopefully track the men who had fired at them.

Kylie kept up with him as the land opened up a bit. Their feet pounded in unison. The spotlight from the chopper revealed men climbing into a car on the American side of the border.

Out of breath, he slowed his pace. They wouldn't be able to catch the men on foot. As if on cue, he heard a car pulling up behind them. Ranger Colt Blackthorn stuck his head out the open window.

"You folks need a ride?"

The car explained the delay in Colt's arrival.

Austin loved that they were such a finely tuned team, that the other rangers knew what the next move would be without being told. Company "E" had sixteen rangers all together. Besides Colt, there were two others on the mission tonight—Brent McCord and Trevor Street, a new hire. Border patrol had provided Kylie and Greg Gunn to assist.

They jumped in, he in the passenger seat and Kylie in the back. Colt hit the accelerator before Austin had even closed the door. He fastened his seat belt. The SUV gained speed, catching air as they bumped along the desolate terrain.

Up ahead, the spotlight from the chopper revealed the car they were pursuing had reached the road.

"They're headed toward that housing development." Kylie's words were iced over with fear.

Austin clenched his teeth. If these were Garcia's men,

they would think nothing of taking the innocent lives of civilians to get away.

Commands flew back and forth on the radios. More ground support consisting of Brent, Trevor and Greg moved into place in a second vehicle.

Colt floored the accelerator. The glowing red taillights of the goons' car burned through Austin. These men weren't going to get away, not on his watch. The car took a sharp turn into the housing development. Colt closed the distance between the two cars. The helicopter loomed above them continuing to spotlight the car that probably contained Garcia's men and maybe even Garcia.

The goon's car took an abrupt turn and disappeared down an alley.

The agent in the chopper kept them updated over the radio. "Suspects have vacated the vehicle. Two to the west, one to the east."

Colt took the turn so sharply it felt like the car was only traveling on two wheels for an instant. Austin's body smashed against the door. He unclipped his seat belt even before the SUV came to a full stop behind the abandoned car.

All three of them jumped out, pulling their handguns from their holsters. No sign of the fugitives. He and Kylie split off to the west while Colt headed in the opposite direction. They moved through the quiet, dark neighborhood.

People were probably still awake—but they were smart enough to switch their lights off and lock their doors after hearing the helicopter. Residents in border towns knew the drill.

A dog barked in the distance. The radio chatter told him other units had moved in quickly as backup. More barking. Maybe one of the K-9 units border patrol utilized was searching for the runners.

Ever alert, he and Kylie slipped along a high wooden fence, both of them turning half circles, weapons drawn. Even with the adrenaline rushing through his system, a strange calm washed over him. He was at his best when the danger level was high. Chalk it up to a childhood that had required constant vigilance in the face of violence, everything he'd been through as a kid made him a good ranger. In his book, he counted that as God's mercy and justice. Only God could redeem a life like his.

The fence ended, and they ducked low as they moved along a hedge. The chopper had left them in the dark, spotlighting something several streets away. Probably Colt's target.

Austin snapped his head around when a noise off to the side caught his attention. Through his goggles, he saw the yellow glow of a man on the run. He watched as the figure headed toward a house set apart from the others. The blast of a gun penetrated the silence and made Austin's heart seize up.

His worst nightmare raised its ugly head. He hated getting civilians involved in this war.

Please, God, don't let the innocent die here tonight.

He'd signed up for this, but the people in these houses hadn't. Kylie surged ahead of him, making a beeline for the house where the goon had gone. As they drew close, she slowed down.

He didn't see any movement outside the house, no shifting shadows. "Maybe he fired to shoot open a door." That was Austin's hope, anyway. That the gun hadn't been used to kill someone.

"I'll take the back. See if I can obtain entry and surprise him." Kylie sprinted into a dead run, disappearing around a corner of the house.

Even as he radioed their location and asked for backup, he knew they couldn't wait for help to arrive. Innocent people might die.

Inside the house, a light flashed on and then off.

Hopefully the goon would just run through the house and Kylie could catch him escaping out the back. That would be a best-case scenario. His chest squeezed tight. Best-case scenarios rarely happened in his line of work.

Heart pounding, Austin made his way to the side of the house. His mind flitted to Kylie as an image of her red hair and bright green eyes flashed across his brain.

Normally, he would assume she could take care of herself, but the death of an informant she clearly cared about had put her off her game, and he wasn't sure if she had recovered.

He purged the thought from his mind. Doubt and hesitation would get them both killed. He had to move in and assume Kylie had his back, just as she always had before.

He found the door that had been blown open by gun blast and slipped inside what turned out to be the garage. He eased open the door that led to the inside of the house. The kitchen was dark. He moved across the tile making no noise at all. Gun drawn, he slipped inside the next room as the floor changed from tile to carpet.

The light in the living room flashed on.

A heavily tattooed Mexican man held a gun to the head of a woman in pajamas. She couldn't be more than thirty. The woman's tear-filled eyes pleaded with him as Garcia's henchman yanked on her long brown hair.

The goon snarled at Austin.

Austin commanded him in Spanish to put the gun down.

The man lifted his chin defiantly. The coldness of the man's eyes told Austin everything he needed to know. This was a seasoned criminal with a heart as cold as ice.

The goon would think nothing of using the woman as a human shield and then killing her so he could get away.

Austin could buy a few precious seconds by talking, but he couldn't take the guy out without risking the woman's life. Everything depended on Kylie moving into place and catching the man off guard.

He prayed she would be able to do that before it was too late.

TWO

Heart pounding against her rib cage, Kylie slipped around the back of the house, searching for entry. An open window caught her eye. It was nothing to push the screen out and slip inside.

She found herself in a dark hallway.

Austin's seemingly calm voice drifted down the hallway. A light was on in what was probably the living room. Though she could not make out what he was saying, she picked up on the thread of tension that twisted tight beneath Austin's words.

She pressed against the wall and moved toward the living room. She heard a second voice, louder than Austin's, switching between broken English and Spanish. The intensity of the tone suggested fear and the threat of violence. She was close enough now to hear some of the words, *"la matare"*: I will kill her.

Terror struck through to Kylie's core, yet she kept moving.

As she drew nearer, she picked up on a third voice, a woman crying and whispering "Please," over and over. Kylie adjusted her grip on her gun and took in a sharp, quick breath.

She was only a few feet from being able to turn the corner into the living room when a door on the opposite end of the hallway swung open. A blonde girl of not more than five stepped out. Her eyes grew wide with fear when she saw Kylie.

Kylie put the gun back in the holster, knowing that was what frightened the child. She placed her finger across her lips indicating that the little girl needed to be quiet.

The girl stayed quiet, but it was clear she didn't trust Kylie from the way she edged toward the living room. Kylie caught her, wedging the child inside her bent arm.

"I need you to go back to your room," Kylie whispered.

"I want my mommy." The girl tried to twist away.

Agitation and the need to stay calm warred within Kylie. She held the child tight but spoke gently even as precious seconds ticked away. "What's your name?" She had to protect this child and that meant taking the time to win the girl's trust.

The girl stopped struggling. "Misty." She took in a jagged sob. "I want my mommy. I can hear her."

"Misty. Everything is going to be all right. I will make sure your mommy is okay."

"Are you the police?" Misty relaxed a little and brushed a strand hair off her face.

"Yes," Kylie said. "I need you to go back to your room and shut the door. Lock it if you can. Can you do that for me, Misty?"

Misty nodded. Kylie released her. The little girl hurried down the carpeted hallway and disappeared back into the room.

Kylie let out a breath, praying that she would be able to keep her word to Misty.

The conversation in the living room had escalated. The henchman swore in Spanish. Austin tried to placate him. "Put the gun down. We don't want to do anything that will send you to jail." Austin spoke in Spanish as he raised his voice.

The words were to let Kylie know that the man was armed.

The woman's crying and pleading grew louder. Kylie knew once she turned the corner she'd have less than a second to take in the scene and make a decision that could save or end a life.

"Don't do this," Austin repeated over and over. Despite the fear he must feel, his voice remained even.

She stepped into the living room as Austin moved toward the goon who held a gun to a woman's head. She had a clean shot at the man's leg. She took it.

The goon cried out, pushed the woman toward Austin as he spun and fired a shot at Kylie. Then he dove for the door, gripping his leg and hopping. Austin froze as the door opened and the goon stepped outside. Intense light flooded the front yard. And Kylie heard gunfire. Backup was here.

Kylie ran toward the woman who was trying to get to her feet. "Get down."

More gunfire outside.

The woman clung to Kylie. "Misty?"

Kylie held the woman in her arms. "She's all right. Your little girl is okay."

Seconds later, lawmen swarmed inside the house. Kylie ignored them as she led the woman down the hall. The door burst open, and Misty ran toward her mom.

The woman wept as she held her daughter. "Oh, baby. My little girl."

Kylie's heart squeezed tight. There was another little girl whose mom wouldn't be coming home tonight… or ever again. Mercedes was only six months old. All night Kylie had played her promise to Valentina over in her mind. Valentina had known the risk she was taking by becoming an informant, and had worried about what that might mean for her daughter. Kylie had given her word that she would take care of Mercedes if anything happened to Valentina. Valentina had put together a plan and made sure the paperwork was in order.

Guilt washed through her. Was the lone figure she'd seen crossing the river right before the gunfire Valentina trying to get to safety? Maybe Valentina had slipped over to Mexico gathering the intel that Garcia had changed locations, and she was trying to find the one person she trusted—Kylie—when she died. Kylie would never know for sure.

Austin came around the corner into the hallway. "Our suspect didn't survive."

With the amount of gunfire, she wasn't surprised. Kylie nodded, but already her mind was on Mercedes.

"Thanks for having my back." Austin's voice was drenched with appreciative warmth.

She met his gaze. For only a moment, he had seemed almost vulnerable, willing to show who he was behind the badge. "It's what we do, right?" No one who worked with Austin on the sixteen-member ranger reconnaissance team had a bad thing to say about him. He did his job and did it well. Yet, to Kylie there seemed to be something almost guarded about him, a part of him that was walled off to the world. The other rangers in company "E" had a nickname for him, Lone Wolf.

Austin squared his broad shoulders and the curtain seemed to fall down around his eyes again. "Right."

The moment of vulnerability had passed quickly.

She'd been drawn to Austin from the first time they'd worked together on another joint task mission. But it was hard to care about a man who buried himself in his work and rarely showed much emotion.

"I guess we get to call it a night." He leaned toward her. "Want to go get a bite to eat? There's an all-night diner just up the road. They have great biscuits and gravy."

On any other night, she would take him up on the invitation. But tonight… "I can't."

His brow furled into a look of confusion and maybe disappointment.

"I have to go into Segundo Barrio tonight."

"Alone, at night? That is a dangerous part of El Paso."

"Valentina—" her heart ached to even say the name "—the woman who died out there tonight has a little girl, six months old. I promised to take care of her if anything happened to her mother."

"Can't it wait?"

"That *T* on Valentina's forehead means they know she was an informant. Mercedes might be in danger too. No, it can't wait." Kylie knew it would be a fool's mission to go by herself. That part of El Paso could be deadly even in broad daylight. Even with all her training, Kylie would be risking her life. But that wouldn't stop her. Already, she felt a strong pull toward Mercedes. The need to protect the little girl seemed to override everything else.

Kylie turned to go.

Austin grabbed her arm. "I smell a trap, Kylie. Did it ever occur to you why Valentina's information was always so golden? She had to have a pretty sweet connection high up."

Feeling a surge of anger, Kylie pulled away. Of course she'd thought of that. But she trusted her instincts. However Valentina got her information, she knew the woman's character. "Valentina was a good person." Whatever she'd been in the past when she lived in Mexico, Valentina had only wanted a better life for herself and her baby.

Austin stepped closer to her. "You go to that part of town tonight alone and there's no guarantee you'll come back."

The familiar twisting and tightening in her gut ate at her resolve. Austin wasn't wrong. That close to Rio Grande even on the American side was ground zero for smuggling humans, guns and drugs from across the border, and all the violence and murder that came along with that.

"Valentina told me she had all the paperwork in place for me to be Mercedes's legal guardian and eventually adopt her," Kylie said. "I have to keep my word."

Austin took a step back and lifted his chin. "Legal guardian? I thought you were just getting the kid to take care of her for a few days until permanent arrangements could be made. Doesn't Valentina have relatives?"

Kylie clenched her jaw. Austin's resistance to her plan was getting under her skin. What business was it of his anyway? "She had no one she could trust. She cut all emotional ties to her past. She played a part and took risks to gather information for me. She wanted the violence to end as badly as I do." She was still reeling from Valentina's death. Her eyes warmed with tears and she turned away. The last thing she needed to do on the job was cry. As one of the few female border patrol agents, she couldn't afford to get a reputation for being soft.

"I was just thinking that maybe it would be easier on the baby for her to go back to Mexico, be with relatives."

"Mercedes was born here in El Paso. Valentina was working on her citizenship. She wanted nothing to do with her lawless family or the baby's father."

Kylie cleared her throat to choke back the tears. "She was a good person who came from a bad place. She was my friend."

Austin's hand cupped her shoulder, warming her through the thin layer of her uniform. His features softened. "I'm sorry. It's none of my business."

She turned to face him, seeing a softness in his expression. "I have to get Mercedes, and it has to be tonight." She hurried toward the door. To her annoyance, Austin was on her heels. This was scary enough, she didn't need him dogging her about her choices. "I'm worried about her safety."

She stepped outside where several agents were still conversing with each other or talking on radios. The ambulance had arrived to haul away the body of the goon who'd been shot.

Misty huddled with her mother on the porch with a blanket over them while an EMT checked them out.

Colt Blackthorn lifted his head from a conversation with another border patrol agent, Greg Gunn. Kylie had worked several missions with Greg. Colt ran toward them.

"Hey, you two. Good teamwork in there." Colt slapped Austin on the back and nodded in Kylie's direction.

Still fuming from her exchange with Austin, Kylie

was grateful for the positive interaction. "So was he one of Garcia's men?" She crossed her arms and shot Austin a look. How could they work so well together and then not get along when the danger was over?

Colt turned slightly toward where the ambulance was loading the body covered in a sheet. He ran a hand over his smooth, dark hair. "More than likely. But we'll have to wait for the ID."

And still no sign of Garcia. Although Kylie was pretty sure he had come across. In all their work together, the information from Valentina had never been bad. Valentina had probably been killed for disclosing where Garcia had planned on coming across.

If Garcia had gotten wind that law enforcement was on to him, he must have changed the location of his crossing at the last minute. Using Valentina's murder as a distraction also served as a message to the brass that Garcia was on to them. Garcia had vowed to kill any lawman that got in his way.

No doubt the rangers with border patrol's help would be focused on figuring out where the drug lord was hiding.

Kylie waited until Colt was out of earshot before turning to face Austin. "I'm going to get that baby. It can't wait."

She whirled away toward one of the border patrol vehicles. Since this wasn't an official mission, she'd have to phone her supervisor at her duty station and get permission to use it. There was no time to go back and retrieve her own car, which would be less conspicuous. She made the call and explained the situation.

When she clicked off her phone, fear and the desire to

do the right thing waged war inside of her as she twisted the key in the ignition and shifted into Reverse.

The passenger side door swung open and Austin jumped in. "It's suicide to go there alone."

Inwardly, she breathed a sigh of relief. Having him along eased her fears. "Fine, go with me, then." Her words tinged with a note of defiance. Not that she would let Austin know she was glad he was along.

He leaned toward her, his tone a little teasing and sarcastic. "I think I will."

Kylie pulled out onto the road and drove through the darkness toward the El Paso neighborhood where she hoped Mercedes was tucked away safely.

After passing several abandoned buildings, Kylie pulled into a gas station. The last thing she wanted to do was run out of gas out there. As she filled the gas tank, the glow of lights in the station and the soft breeze on her skin calmed her. She knew it was a false sense of security. She touched her gun in its holster. She was trained to deal with violence and the unexpected. But this time, a baby's safety was at stake.

Austin rolled down the window. "You want me to do the driving? One less thing you got to think about."

The tension coiling through her chest eased up a bit. Austin's presence and solid instincts had that effect on her when they were working together. But this wasn't work. The mission was personal. And he was still here to support her. That made her like him even more. "That sounds like a great idea." She tossed him the keys.

She slipped into the passenger seat and gave him Valentina's address. Kylie had never been to Valentina's place. That would have been too risky. When Valentina had information for her, they met in busy public places.

But this was the plan they had discussed for the worst-case scenario. Valentina wanted this plan in place almost from the time she had approached Kylie about being an informant. Kylie's heart ached over the loss of her friend.

"Lot of gang activity in that part of town," he said as they pulled into traffic.

She nodded. Not everyone there was a criminal, though. Like Valentina, so many were just people trying to get by and raise their families, unable to afford anything safer.

They passed city streets where men and women spilled out from bars, some of them standing around, some of them fighting. The glow of neon lights flashed across the windshield. Tension knotted through her as gunfire sounded in the distance. She couldn't have done this alone. "Thank you for coming with me."

"How did you meet your informant?"

A heaviness settled into her chest as the memories flooded through her mind. "At church."

He nodded. "Do you both sing in the choir?"

"How did you know I sing in the choir?" It was Kylie's turn to do a double take. "We go to the same church?"

"I sit in the back. I leave right when the service is over." He grinned as he stared straight ahead. "Yeah, I'm one of those guys." Austin was a serious man who rarely smiled. His whole face lit up when he did. "The back-bench dweller, that's me."

"The important thing is that you go," Kylie said. This side of Austin was a surprise. At work, he came across as a confident man who knew his job and did it well, but he never talked about personal matters. She hadn't even realized he was a believer. So they'd been going to the same church all this time. Maybe in social settings he was a much shyer man.

"Guess I feel a little out of place at church." He leaned closer to the windshield, probably looking for a street name. "You sit in the same seat every Sunday though, after you're done singing. Creature of habit."

So he had noticed her at church. She wanted to ask him why he felt out of place, but as private as he was, it would probably be too probing a question. "You should say hi to me sometime instead of just staring at the back of my head."

Austin nodded and let out a one-syllable laugh.

They passed several buildings with murals painted on them—something this part of town was famous for.

Austin turned down a street that had no streetlights. The pavement changed to dirt road. The area consisted of rundown adobe houses and two apartment buildings that looked badly in need of repair. Some of the windows were boarded up, shot out or had gang symbols graffiti all over them. One man came to the door and watched them as they rolled by, his gaze as cold as steel. Most people probably hid inside at this hour, doors bolted against the violence.

Kylie pointed. "It must be the apartment building at the end of the street."

Loud music with an intense bass beat erupted from a side street. Austin eased the car off the road, turned off the ignition and killed the lights.

"Stay down," he said. "This could be fine, but let's not take any chances."

THREE

Kylie crouched down below the dashboard. Driving the border patrol vehicle only made them a bigger target in this neighborhood. Her hand brushed over her gun as her pulse thudded in her eardrums. If they were faced with gang activity, they would not have the firepower to get out alive.

Austin kept his head low, as well. The music swelled to full volume. The whole street seemed to be pounding. The vibrations shook their car. Through the open window, she heard the dissonant harmony of men verbally jousting with each other in Spanish. A single gunshot echoed along the street.

Austin rolled the window up. The windows had wire mesh on them to protect them when people threw rocks at them, which happened a lot. But that wouldn't prevent them from being dragged out into the street and shot.

Kylie flinched at the gunshot but maintained her composure.

Austin peered above the dashboard. "Just shooting in the air." His voice never lost that calming tone. "Showing off their machismo."

They waited for what seemed like forever until the

music and the drunken conversation died away altogether. The men must have gone inside one of the buildings.

Austin sat back up and drove the car forward toward the building where little Mercedes was being kept safe… she hoped.

He shifted into Park. "Let's make this fast." They got out of the car. They were so close to the border, Kylie could hear the traffic rushing by on the Cesar Chavez Highway.

"She's on the second floor. Apartment twenty-seven." Valentina had an arrangement with an older woman named Doris to watch the baby while she was at classes. Hopefully, that was who was with the baby now.

They hurried into the building past the debris of old newspapers, heaping plastic bags, broken toys. Kylie's heart raced as she took the stairs two at a time. Austin came up behind her. She stood in front of apartment twenty-seven. She knocked twice. No answer.

She turned the knob and called inside as fear gripped her heart. She dared not cry out, just in case someone with ill intent waited inside. What if they were too late? What if the same people who killed Valentina had already gone after her baby?

She stepped across the threshold. Austin had already drawn his weapon. The kitchen was run-down but neat. Clean dishes were stacked in the cupboards with no doors. The worn linoleum floor was mopped. There was something poignant about the Thanksgiving centerpiece in the middle of the table. Sorrow washed over Kylie. Valentina had really tried to make a nice home for her baby.

Kylie drew her attention to a pattern of holes on the wall, a spray of bullets. Her throat went tight.

Austin cupped her shoulder. "Those bullet holes could have been there for years."

How was he able to pick up on her distress like that?

She turned a slow half circle, looking for hiding places. *Please, God, let that little girl be here and safe.*

The apartment was small. She saw a closed door off to the right that must be a bedroom. She pulled her gun as she made her way toward it. Austin stayed close.

She eased the door open. The room consisted of a mat and blankets on the floor next to a stack of textbooks. There was no sign of a crib or basket for a baby.

"We have to find that little girl. I'm not going to break my promise to Valentina."

"Sometimes in dangerous neighborhoods, people have hiding places." Austin paced the perimeter of the room, stopping to stare at the closet. He tapped on the walls until the sound changed inside the closet. He leaned in, pulling a thin panel out of place.

Kylie saw what was probably a hot water heater. She pulled her flashlight from her belt just as a baby's cry erupted in the darkness. Her heart surged with joy at the sound. She shone the light on a gray-haired woman holding a bundle wrapped in a pink blanket.

Kylie spoke in Spanish. "Doris, right? Valentina told me about you. I'm Kylie."

The woman still looked frightened. She replied, speaking so rapidly in Spanish her words seemed to be stacked on top of each other. She said something about men banging on the door looking for Valentina.

Kylie leaned in and held out her arms. "It's okay now."

Doris rose to her feet, still holding the baby. "Valentina?"

Kylie shook her head. "She didn't make it." The pain

of the loss hit Kylie all over again. Her stomach tied into knots.

Though clearly upset, Doris placed the bundle in Kylie's arms. Kylie stared down at deep brown eyes and rosebud lips. She felt as though warm honey were dripping over her. Those eyes. So filled with trust. Would she be able to take care of someone so helpless?

The baby brushed her fingers under Kylie's chin. Mercedes knew Kylie. Valentina had brought her to their meetings when she couldn't get a sitter, and Kylie watched her in early service when she had nursery duty.

Not taking her eyes off of Mercedes, Kylie stepped back so Doris could get out.

The woman continued to talk, waving her hands, telling more about how the men had frightened her. She gathered a bag up off the floor and placed it in Austin's hands saying a single word. *"Papa?"*

Kylie felt her cheeks flush. For some reason, Doris had thought she and Austin were a couple. "No, he's just a friend." She locked Austin in her gaze. He looked equally embarrassed. Just a very good friend.

Austin examined the contents of the bag. "It looks like baby clothes and paperwork giving you legal custody of the baby. A judge probably has to sign off on it."

Kylie held Mercedes close to her chest. The child's silky smooth cheek rubbed against her own as Kylie felt the warmth of the little body. She breathed in a prayer that she would be able to take care of Mercedes.

Doris pointed at a baby bag with ducks carrying umbrellas on it. Austin picked the second bag up, carrying both bags in one hand. Doris, who was probably not more than four feet tall, hurried over to Kylie.

She stood on tiptoe to kiss Mercedes's forehead. "*Mi dulce bebé*. God will take care of you."

Through the open window, another car playing loud music trolled the neighborhood. Doris's features grew tight with fear as she hurried toward the door and out into the hallway.

"I'm with her. Let's get out of here. This place makes me nervous," said Austin, drawing his gun.

They ran toward the door, down the stairs and out into the night. A gunshot resounded, knocking plaster off the fence wall in front of them. Austin stepped close to Kylie. His gun was at the ready as he searched the roofs of the apartment buildings.

"I want to believe that was random. But if men came looking for Valentina, we can't take any chances. Maybe they want to hurt her kid too."

Clutching a crying Mercedes, Kylie raced to the car. Even before they got to the curb, Kylie could see that the car's tires had been flattened.

Holding Mercedes even tighter, she pushed past her fear. She had a baby to think about. "What are we going to do?"

Austin paced three strides in one direction and three strides in the other. "Let's just keep walking. Standing around makes us look too vulnerable. I'll call one of the other rangers to meet us as soon as he can."

Kylie tried to ignore the rising panic that made it hard to breath. Heart pounding, fear raging, she started walking. No matter what threat of violence was out there, she had to get this baby to a safe place.

Adrenaline flooded through Austin, making him alert and ready to act. Just as he was putting the bags down to reach for his phone another shot whizzed past them and embedded in the metal of the car. Austin edged closer to Kylie and the baby, directing them toward the shelter of a building with an overhang.

Austin glanced all around. Where were those shots coming from, anyway? "I don't think that shot was random."

"You think they are targeting us?"

He stared at Kylie holding the bundled baby. Maybe it was because they were law enforcement or maybe it all connected back to Kylie's informant. Either way, they were in danger.

They didn't have a lot of options. "Yes. Let's keep moving." Austin felt like he couldn't get a deep breath. What had they gotten themselves into? "I'm going to phone in what has happened, make arrangements for this car to be brought back before it's stripped for parts and see if I can get someone to meet us."

Resting the bag handles in his elbow, Austin maintained pace with her while calling his supervisor, Major Thomas Vance. As he explained their situation, he felt a heaviness he didn't understand. He was responsible for Kylie and the little life she held in her arms. He could handle a firefight no problem, but a woman and a baby depending on him made him weak in the knees.

They hurried past abandoned buildings and others painted with colorful murals depicting scenes from the Bible and famous Mexicans.

A man jumped out in front of them, his eyes wide and round.

Austin stepped between the man and Kylie, squaring his shoulders and offering his move-it-along look, furled eyebrows, chest out, hand hovering over his weapon.

The man hung his head and stumbled away into the darkness.

More people appeared in doorways as they drew near to a paved street. Because they were law enforcement, they were viewed with suspicion in a neighborhood so close to the border. It made them vulnerable to attack. Them… and the precious cargo in Kylie's arms.

Guilt gripped his chest. He didn't like the idea of putting the baby in so much danger. They would have been okay if they could've jumped in the car and left the neighborhood quickly.

The dirt road turned into pavement again. The orange glow of lights increased as did the traffic whizzing by on the streets.

Kylie's gaze darted everywhere looking for threats as she held the baby close to her chest.

Austin put his phone away. "Brent, one of the other rangers, will meet us on South Mesa Street," Austin said. "We only have to walk a few more blocks."

"Right now that feels like a million miles." Though she spoke in an even tone, Austin picked up on the terror threaded through her words.

He put his hand on her elbow. "Just keep moving."

He appreciated that Kylie seemed to have nerves of steel even if she might be afraid on the inside. He felt it too. It was unsettling thinking about the bad things that might happen to the baby and to them.

"It's not that much farther," he said, hoping to sound reassuring.

A car squealed its brakes. Both of them instinctively jumped a little closer to the brick building—not that it would provide any protection. There was no safe zone here. People could come at them from the street. Men could bring a car up to the curb and snatch them. Someone could shoot them from a distant building.

The shots back at the apartment building bothered him most of all. He was sure they'd been targeted deliberately, but why? Was it just because they were law enforcement?

Under normal circumstances, this would have been exciting, but not with the baby to think about. Why had Kylie agreed to such a crazy thing? Raising a kid by herself. He had to admire the size of her heart, but still. She was a border patrol agent, which meant long crazy hours. Had she really thought this thing through?

He could see the lights of a busy thoroughfare up ahead. "Brent should be waiting there for us. Just up ahead."

He hoped his words helped calm Kylie. If she was tense, Mercedes might pick up on it and get upset. Or were babies not that perceptive? He wasn't sure. He didn't know anything about babies or families.

Austin had never known his biological father, and his childhood hadn't offered many decent examples. He'd been four when his older sister died in a car accident. His mother, overwhelmed with guilt because she'd been driving, developed a drinking problem that caused them to move often. Unless he counted the string of violent boyfriends his mother attached herself to—the best of which ignored him, and the worst of which were actively cruel to him—he had no frame of reference for what it meant to be a dad or a husband.

Gunshots sounded behind them. More squealing tires. More racing cars. He heard a car with a loud motor zoom up behind them. The owner revved the engine.

Austin wrapped an arm around Kylie and the baby and pulled them toward the shadows of the building.

Men got out of the car and paced the street. Some were shirtless, revealing gang tattoos and the guns shoved into their waistbands. Austin didn't bother looking around to see if there was anyone he could appeal to for help.

If any violence erupted in this neighborhood, the people around here would just look the other way.

Mercedes cried. Kylie shushed her and bounced a little.

One of the men stepped toward Kylie and Austin, fixating on the baby.

"Ah, gringo, you have a *niña bonita* with you." He tilted his head as his voice filled with menace. "Out here in the cold night."

"We don't want any trouble." But despite his words, Austin was looking for an opening to land a good punch. So much of fighting was about psychology—especially with a group like this. If Austin seemed weak, they'd fall on him like vultures. But if he seemed strong, he and Kylie might be all right. Sizing up his opponent, Austin decided he could handle this guy.

The man looked down his nose at them and narrowed his eyes in a threatening way.

Austin landed a single blow to the man's stomach that doubled him over. The other men took several steps back, raising their hands in a surrender motion as Austin directed Kylie and the baby back toward the edge of the sidewalk.

"Well, that takes care of that." A note of amusement danced through Kylie's words as they hurried along.

"Sometimes quick and clean is best. We don't have time to play diplomat with thugs. We need to get this kid to a safe place."

Kylie stopped and looked Austin directly in the eyes. "Yes, *we* do."

Maybe it was just the light, but he thought he saw admiration, maybe even affection, in her eyes. He kept walking. Yeah, it was probably just the way the light was hitting her face. Someone like Kylie wouldn't be interested in someone like him. She probably had Thanksgiving with twenty relatives around and lots of laughter. He spent his holidays at the retirement home with the former cop who had been his saving grace. Robert Wilson had been his parole officer when he was fourteen and in trouble. Old Bob had seen a potential in Austin that he hadn't seen in himself. Since his mother's death, Old Bob was the closest thing to family Austin had.

He shook his head. Why was he even entertaining thoughts about Kylie?

Kylie looked up at him. "Why are you shaking your head?"

"No reason." His cheeks flushed with heat.

"Talking to yourself because it's the only time you can have an intelligent conversation?"

He laughed. "Yes, that must be it."

He had no idea she had such a great sense of humor. Chalk it up to the tense situation. Just one of those things you learn by helping someone rescue a baby out of a bad neighborhood.

Kylie bounced the baby. She pressed her lips together as she looked up ahead. "Where is he? Where is Brent?"

Austin scanned the street. "He'll get here as fast as he can."

Another car with music pounding eased past them. The back window rolled down and one of the gang members sneered at them, forming his finger into a gun and pointing it at him. The car sped up as the gang member rolled up the tinted window.

Austin's chest squeezed tight as though it were in a vise. They could not stand around waiting for long.

Up ahead he saw one of the ranger vehicles park along the curb. Brent McCord got out and leaned against it, offering them a quick nod of recognition. They were safe.

Austin glanced over beside him to the auburn-haired woman and her blanketed bundle. Tension knotted at the back of his neck. Maybe the shots at the apartment building had not been personal and had been aimed at them only because of their uniforms. He hoped that was the case. The other possibility was far too worrying.

Garcia's contacts were abundant on both the American and Mexican side of the border. If Garcia wanted them dead, he would see to it they were taken out.

FOUR

Kylie could feel the fatigue settle into her muscles as she and Austin rode horses through a remote part of the desert. The last twenty-four hours had been a whirlwind of getting Mercedes settled in and starting the legal process for adoption. Kylie's neighbor, an older woman named Gloria Espina who she'd known for years, agreed to watch the baby for now. Kylie had put in a request to be moved to more monitoring work once the Garcia mission was complete. The risk to her well-being in that position would be much lower than going out on patrol.

Austin put the binoculars up to his eyes. "What have we here?"

In the fading light, she could see the glint of metal in the distance, a vehicle of some sort.

Austin had requested to work with her again. Two teams consisting of a ranger and border agent had gone out to search the desert for where Garcia might have crossed over. Colt Blackthorn and Greg Gunn had taken a section of land to the east.

She was glad she'd been paired with Austin. They were both invested in finding Garcia. They would need to see this case to the end…together. And yet she hadn't told him about her request to be put on more monitoring work after the case closed. There hadn't been much conversation between them at all. It hurt her feelings that they'd been on duty for a couple of hours and Austin hadn't asked anything about Mercedes. She was struggling with her own doubts. His support would be nice.

She pulled out her binoculars. "No sign of activity." This could be the van Garcia had used to get across.

"All the same, let's move in slow." Austin slipped off his horse.

The rougher terrain and the need to be quiet made horses the better option in this remote part of desert. Growing up a ranch kid had served her well in that before she'd even trained as an agent, she knew how to ride and shoot.

Mexican surveillance cameras had photographed the van with a passenger who looked like Garcia. Now it was up to them to figure out if they were on the right trail. The van was generic in appearance, favored by the cartels for that reason.

Kylie caught movement out of the corner of her eye. She whirled around but saw nothing.

"Something wrong?"

In the desert twilight, she could have just been seeing things. Still, she hadn't been able to shake the feeling that they were being watched.

Trust your instincts.

That's what her training told her.

She dismounted. "I'm not sure."

"I sense it too," said Austin. "It looks quiet. But something feels like it could explode in our faces."

They moved in slowly, stopping to watch the area around the van and in the hills that surrounded them.

Both of them dropped to the ground, scanning the landscape with vigilance. The driver's side door was flung open. Someone had made a speedy retreat.

After several minutes of seeing no movement or potential threats, they closed in.

Austin reached for the handle on the back door of the van. Kylie held her breath. It wasn't unusual for coyotes, men who transported Mexicans across the border for a fee, to leave people to die if they feared getting caught.

The door wasn't locked. That was a good sign.

Kylie pulled her gun while Austin flung the door open.

She let out her breath, whispering a prayer of gratitude when there were no dead bodies, no rotting stench.

Austin crawled inside, shining his light all over. "Let's see if we can find anything that indicates this is the van Garcia came over in."

Vans like this were used all the time by cartels for a variety of reasons. It would be a waste of manpower for Forensics to go over it if it couldn't be clearly and directly linked to a crime, preferably directly to Garcia. Kylie crawled in as well, lifting seat cushions and checking the glove compartment. Chances were the van was stolen, so tracking it back to the owner might be a dead end.

Again she thought she spotted a flash of light out of the corner of her eye, but when she stared through the windshield, she saw only the bushes and hills behind them. Her heart beat a little faster. She talked to calm her nerves. "So have there been any more sightings of Garcia's sister, the one he wants dead?"

Austin pulled a panel out of the van and shone his light inside it. "Nothing new. We know Adriana got across the border. We know she's hiding from her brother. All of that we know because of Carmen." Austin's voice faltered at the mention of the female ranger's name.

Carmen Alvarez was deeply embedded in the Garcia drug cartel. After relaying the message about the date—but not the location—of Garcia's crossing, Carmen had not been in communication with the team. Kylie knew the other rangers were worried about their fellow officer. It had been Valentina who had provided them with the place of Garcia's crossing. Her one last courageous act.

"I've got drug residue in here." Austin rubbed his fingers together. "That's enough to take it in. Even if it doesn't link back to Garcia, it could open something up on a different case."

Austin jumped out of the van.

Kylie climbed out as well, remembering something she'd noticed in one of the surveillance photos. She moved toward the back bumper of the van. "The paint is scraped off here just like in the photo."

In the dusk of evening, Austin shone his flashlight on where Kylie pointed. "Good work. I'd say this was the van Garcia used." He clicked off his light and turned a half circle. "Let's see if we can figure out where these guys went."

Kylie located the tracks leading away from the van. "Three men, steady and quick in their steps. Headed northeast." She increased her pace, still shining the light on the ground. "I wonder when they got picked up. If it was Garcia, I can't see him suffering the indignity of walking too far." She hurried toward the brush where some of the grass had been flattened. "Looks like they sat down to wait about here."

She loved this part of the job, reading the tracks. At the academy, they called it cutting sign, a skill border patrol picked up from Native American tribes.

Lights flashed off to the side, unmistakable this time. Gunfire cut through the night. Kylie's eardrums hurt from the blast coming so close to her. Austin's arms went around her, leading her away from the brush and the direction the shot had come from.

Both of them dove to the ground and crawled commando-style toward the horses. Another shot whizzed over them close to Kylie.

Kylie's heart raged against her rib cage. She could see the silhouette of the horses up ahead. More gunfire tore up the ground in front of her. She gasped but kept moving.

They were close enough to hear the metal bridle parts clinking as the horses, agitated by the shots, jerked their heads up and down. Kylie and Austin rose to their feet and sprinted the remaining distance.

Both of them mounted up and spurred the horses into a gallop. Off to the side, she saw the lights from someone following them on an ATV.

Another rifle shot zinged through the air. Kylie's horse reared up. She held on, tightening the reins. More gunfire. The horse reared again and overbalanced, falling to the ground. Kylie's leg was pinned under the weight of the animal.

The roar of the approaching ATV assaulted her ears.

She fought to free herself as the horse struggled to get back up. The horse got to its feet and galloped away, uninjured but frightened by the gunfire.

Austin helped her to stand. She was on autopilot as she rose to her feet. Her leg hurt, but she didn't think anything was broken. An image of Mercedes's sweet face flashed through her head. She had to stay alive for that baby.

Austin had already mounted up again. He held out his hand. "Why is he only shooting at you?"

"I'm not sure." She stuck her foot in the stirrup and swung on behind him wrapping her arms around his waist.

There was no time to radio in. This spot was far away from everything and everyone. Backup couldn't get out here fast enough anyway. They were on their own with an assassin nipping at their heels.

As Kylie's arms wrapped tight around his waist, Austin could hear the ATV gaining on them. The guy was using a rifle and clearly had some sniper skills, but he'd have to stop to touch off another round. Aiming a rifle required two free hands.

Plus, shooting a moving target from another moving target would be a challenge even for a highly trained sniper.

If the guy was willing to hunt them down like this, the assault wasn't just about scaring them away from the van.

In the fading light, Austin scanned the terrain up ahead. The horse could go places where an ATV would struggle. He headed toward the foothills where the ground would be rocky. The nimble horse skirted through the boulders.

Kylie rested her head against his shoulder. Judging from how tightly she held on, she was still afraid. Like the good agent she was, she held it together. The sound of the ATV dimmed as he made his way into deeper, thicker brush.

He could no longer hear the ATV, but that didn't mean the man wasn't tracking them on foot. The man had either been lying in wait by the van or had followed them out, waiting for the time when they were most vulnerable and farthest away from backup for a targeted killing. All the more reason to think the van was most likely used by Garcia.

The horse slowed as anything resembling a trail disappeared. The thick brush hid them well but also made it hard to make progress.

Austin dismounted and pulled the horse along. His ears tuned in to every sound.

"I should get down too," Kylie said. "The tall brush provides some cover."

Austin nodded. It bothered him that the shooter had only fired at Kylie as though this was personal. Carmen had told the team that Garcia had vowed to kill any ranger or agent who got in his way. Why hadn't this sniper taken shots at him, too?

Something rustled in the brush behind them. Kylie pressed close to him. The noise died away. Could be a nocturnal animal.

They worked their way through the brush and out into the open desert before radioing for help. When he glanced over his shoulder, he saw intermittent lights moving toward them from where they had just escaped. They were still being pursued.

"We better mount up. Help will meet us at the road."

Kylie swung on again. The warmth of her touch permeated his shirt where she wrapped her arms around him.

"Watch behind us and let me know if he's getting too close. We'll find a hiding place and ambush him." He spurred the horse into a gallop. They rode hard until the horse tired, and he slowed into a canter.

After some time had passed, Kylie spoke over his

shoulder. "I don't see lights anymore. He must have given up."

A ranger with a horse trailer came to pick them up just as morning light warmed the desert.

They waited at the ranch where the ranger horses were kept for their ride into town. Though it was the ranch hand's job, Kylie insisted on cooling down the mount that had served them so well.

He watched her brush the animal as the morning sun caught the coppery highlights in her auburn hair. She spoke soothingly to the horse.

"Any news on the other horse?" She stroked the mane. Her voice was tinged with sadness.

"They'll send someone else to look for him. He was in good enough shape to run off. I don't think he was hit, just frightened. They should find him."

Kylie led the horse out to the corral. She was a natural with them. He was a city boy who had grown up on a skateboard. Riding was a skill he had had to learn for the job. She slapped the animal's back flank and he galloped away.

She came to stand beside Austin where he rested one foot on the lower rung of the wooden corral.

Another long night over for both of them. Their work felt a lot like two steps forward and one step back. He was glad to make those steps with someone as good at her job as Kylie. At least they'd found the van.

A dust cloud up the road told him their ride had arrived.

Colt Blackthorn rolled down the window and rested his elbow on it. "You two again. We have to stop meeting like this." The breeze ruffled his dark hair. "Heard you guys did better than Greg and I. Good job finding the van."

Kylie climbed into the front seat and Austin got in the back. As they drove away, Kylie glanced out the back window. "Hey look, it looks like the other horse came in on his own."

Austin checked his side-view mirror to see a ranch hand leading their runaway horse to the corral.

"They always know their way back to where the food is," Kylie said.

They drove for several miles on a dirt road.

"How's that new baby of yours?" Colt offered Kylie a warm smile.

The ride into town consisted of Kylie talking about every nuance of her hours with Mercedes. Her voice took on a light lilting quality.

Austin felt like he was a stranger in a foreign land. He didn't understand a mother's joy in talking about her child. He supposed his mother had loved him before the accident and before the drinking, but those memories were covered over by the years that followed.

He leaned forward in the seat. "Drop Kylie off first. I want to make sure she gets home safe and sound to that little girl." His voice sounded a little stiff. As happy as he was for Kylie, he just wasn't sure how she was going to be able to do her job and be a mom.

Kylie's apartment complex was in a middle-class neighborhood next to a park. Kylie phoned ahead telling her babysitter that she was on her way.

Kylie nearly jumped out of the car as Colt pulled up to the curb.

Austin got out and climbed into the front seat. He peered in the rearview mirror at the scene unfolding behind him. The sitter, an older woman, had come outside pushing a baby stroller with Mercedes in it. He had to admit, the sight of that sweet baby face and round brown eyes had tugged at his heart the first time he'd seen Mercedes.

As Colt gained speed, something else in the mirror caught Austin's eye. He craned his head. There it was, the glint of a rifle on top of the apartment building. A sniper with his sights set on Kylie.

When she was a few feet from Kylie, Mrs. Espina leaned over to unbuckle Mercedes from her stroller.

Kylie's heart leaped when Mercedes kicked her legs with glee.

"That's my little girl. You make coming home that much sweeter." The bright eyes tugged at Kylie's heart as her voice grew sadder. "I wish your mom was here. I know you must miss her even if you don't totally understand what happened."

The sound of squealing tires caught her attention.

She looked over to see Austin and Colt turning around in the road at a high speed. Something was wrong. Her heart seized up as she hit the ground and crawled toward Mercedes to protect her.

She heard the rifle shots nanoseconds before she covered Mercedes with her body.

She couldn't put Gloria at risk. "Mrs. Espina, run, get to your apartment." The older woman backed up and then hurried away. No shots were fired at her.

Kylie gathered the baby in her arms.

Austin was beside her almost instantly, lifting her while she held the baby, directing her toward the cover of the building.

She caught a flash of Colt running toward the neighboring building, probably to apprehend the shooter.

"Where do you live?" Austin's voice was in her ear.

The question clarified her fuzzy thinking, and she answered as she kept running. Mercedes cried as she pressed herself against Kylie's chest. Kylie raced toward her apartment. Once inside, her only thought was to comfort Mercedes.

Austin paced the room then drew back the curtains to peek outside.

A moment later, Austin's phone rang.

"Yes, Colt." Austin drew the curtain back again still looking for threats.

Austin listened for a moment, nodding. "Thanks." He listened some more. "Let us know. We're in apartment fourteen."

He clicked off his phone and turned to face Kylie. "Colt couldn't catch him, but he saw which way the guy ran. The police have been called. There'll be half a dozen cops looking for him."

"So he's still out there." Still fighting her own agitation and fear, Kylie bounced Mercedes and made soothing noises. No child should be put through that kind of incident. Especially after the trauma of losing her mom.

Austin stepped closer to her. "I think this is personal, Kylie. Someone wants you dead."

Mercedes stopped crying. Her soft fingers brushed over Kylie's neck as she grabbed her collar to hold on to. While a thousand conflicting emotions tumbled through Kylie's mind, the only clear thought was that she wanted to keep Mercedes safe. Mercedes stuck two fingers in her mouth and stared up at Kylie, a look of total trust in her eyes.

"I think you need to put that kid in protective custody so you can do your job and resolve this threat," Austin said.

Kylie couldn't believe what she was hearing. "So I can do my job?" Was that what mattered the most to him?

Austin paced. His hand gestures indicated he was rattled. "Both of you could have died out there." What was going on with him, anyway? He was Mr. Cool under Fire. She'd never seen him this upset.

"I know that. Don't you think I know that?" Kylie wrestled with even more doubt. More than anything she wanted to keep Mercedes safe, but the thought of being separated from her nearly broke her in half. She was the one who could best protect her, and the shots had been fired at *her*, not at the baby. Was the little girl really in danger if she stayed? Mercedes had lost her mother. Turning her over to strangers would only add trauma onto trauma. Her insides twisted from the turmoil she felt. Austin was right though, something bad could have happened to Mercedes.

He combed his fingers through his dark blond hair. "We need to get Garcia, and we need to get whoever shot at you. Chances are, they're connected."

"We?" Her jaw tightened. It was clear he was uncomfortable with her new status as a single mother. He just wanted her to be Kylie, unattached, trusted border patrol agent, focused on nothing more than the job. But that wasn't her anymore. She was a mother now. Didn't he understand that? This was hard enough. Why couldn't he support her?

Still agitated, Kylie rose to her feet to get Mercedes's bottle. She settled into her overstuffed recliner and stared down at Mercedes's rich brown eyes. Little fingers wrapped around the bottle. The steady rhythm of the baby's sucking soothed her rankled spirit.

"Putting her somewhere safe until this is over would be the best thing for her." Austin's voice was a little softer.

Kylie fumed. The best thing for Mercedes, or the best thing for Austin and his work?

There was a knock on the door and Colt stuck his head in. "The locals caught him. He's an American. They will turn him over to us for questioning by tomorrow morning."

Through the open door, Kylie could see Mercedes's stroller out in the courtyard knocked over on its side. She shuddered at what could have happened…if Austin hadn't been here. She didn't appreciate the pressure Austin was putting on her, but he had a point about the danger, and she wanted to do the right thing for Mercedes.

Colt left. Austin closed the door. He turned to face her. "You want to be there for the interrogation, don't you?"

Kylie felt like Austin was asking her a much bigger question.

Which are you going to be, a mom or a border control agent?

FIVE

Austin turned to look at the uniformed officer as he stood facing the one-way glass where the sniper suspect was being questioned. "What do we know about this guy?"

The officer looked at his clipboard. "Mark Smith. Veteran. Sniper training. PTSD. Minor scuffles with the law."

"What did he say was his reason for taking shots at the off-duty border patrol agent?" Austin stared at the distraught man combing his fingers through his disheveled hair. He didn't look like a hardened criminal. More like a desperate man trying to get by. "Let me guess. Someone paid him."

"Yes, though we haven't been able to nail down who," said the officer. "We showed him a picture of Garcia. He said that wasn't the guy."

Austin leaned a little closer to the glass. "That doesn't mean anything. Garcia rarely does his own dirty work."

"Mark was pretty broken up about there being a child out there. I think he might talk. I suppose that is where you come in. Do you want to take a crack at him?"

Austin checked his watch. Kylie was late. She was never late. "I guess this can't wait forever."

"It doesn't hurt to let a suspect sweat for a while alone in an interrogation room," said the officer.

The door burst open and Kylie stepped inside. "I'm here. I had to wait for the sitter to show up." She wasn't walking with the usual bounce in her step, and she had dark circles under her eyes.

"You look tired," said Austin.

"Mercedes had a tough night. She's still getting used to her new surroundings…and to me." She crossed her arms. "I'm sure she misses her mother."

How much help was she going to be in the interrogation if she was worn out?

"Glad you made it." A little note of irritation slipped into his voice. He hadn't intended that. Her personal life was her personal life. Why couldn't he let this go?

She flicked him a quick look before squaring her shoulders and staring through the one-way glass. "So tell me what we know so far."

Austin repeated what the officer had told him. "We can maybe find out if this guy links back to the Garcia investigation."

"Okay, let's do this." Kylie seemed to be perking up.

The officer turned and picked a binder up off a table. He handed it to Kylie. "Garcia's known associates."

The binder had to be four inches thick. "Garcia knows a lot of people. Talk about being a social butterfly."

"He is the belle of the ball," Kylie said.

Austin laughed. The joke seemed to break the tension between them and remind him of why he liked working with her so much.

He opened the door to the interrogation room. He entered first with Kylie behind him.

Mark Smith rested his elbows on the table and stared

down. His long brown hair fell over his face. Kylie took a seat, but Austin remained standing. The positioning wasn't an accident. Standing gave him superiority over the suspect. By sitting, Kylie came across as the approachable one.

Mark Smith looked up. His expression turned a little guilty when he saw Kylie.

Recognition spread across his face. "You're the lady." His voice tinged with shame.

"Yes, I'm the one." Her voice was soft and filled with compassion. Anyone else who was sitting three feet away from the man who had taken a shot at her might have shown fear, but not Kylie.

Mark began to shake his head as his eyes glazed. "I don't know what I was thinking. I got bills and…a habit. I wasn't told there would be a kid involved."

At first, Austin wasn't sure if bringing Kylie in for this questioning would be smart, but it seemed to have the effect he was hoping for. Mark Smith had not given much up under police questioning, but facing the woman who had been his target revealed that he had a conscience. Maybe now they could get some useful information out of him.

"Mark, we can get you a much lighter sentence if you help us identify the man who hired you," Kylie said.

Mark sat back in his chair and gripped the edge of the table. "I don't know if I can. It was dark in the bar, and I had already had a couple of drinks."

Kylie pushed the binder toward him.

"I've looked at those already," Mark said.

Austin stopped pacing and crossed his arms over his chest. "We'd like you to try again." If Kylie was the voice of caring, he was the one who represented strength. It was their personal version of good cop, bad cop.

Mark closed his eyes and let out a heavy breath. "Like I said, it was dark and my memory doesn't work right." He shifted in his seat, opened his eyes and stared at the ceiling. "The guy had a tattoo on his neck and one on his hand."

Austin stepped a little closer to the table. That was more information than the police had been able to get.

"Do you remember what the tattoo was of?" Kylie kept her voice even to give the message that there was no pressure in remembering. In fact, countless lives might depend on them finding the connection back to Garcia.

Mark turned in his chair as though he was going to get up. Austin braced in case the suspect was about to erupt. Austin's first instinct was to move toward Kylie.

"Mark?" Kylie remained still, her voice like a soothing stream.

Mark turned back around. "I hate myself for what I did." He buried his face in his hands. "It's the drugs… I'm so sorry."

Kylie leaned forward and scooted her hand across the table close to but not touching Mark's hand. "I forgive you."

Mark raised his head and stared at her for a long moment. The only noise in the room was the whir of a fan in the wall. "You really mean that, don't you?"

Kylie nodded. She kept her gaze on Mark as tears pooled in her own eyes.

"This is not the man I ever wanted to be." Mark's whole demeanor seemed to soften.

"I know that," said Kylie.

A silence enveloped the three of them. The quiet felt almost sacred. Austin remembered stepping into a church as a troubled teenager demanding that if God was real, He better show Himself. This moment felt just as heavy.

Mark rocked back and forth. "I'll help you as much as I can. I don't care if I go to jail or not."

"We'll do the best to make sure you get the help you need, Mark," Austin said.

"The police have a computer program that has all the known gang tattoos. You can look at that to see if it jars your memory," Kylie said.

The program would also match the type of tattoo to a specific cartel member if he was in the system. Identifying the tattoos was a huge step in the right direction.

Mark nodded. He sat up a little straighter and made eye contact with both Kylie and Austin. The change in him was night and day.

"Did the man who hired you say anything that would help us figure out who he was? Did he use any names?"

Mark rested his palms on the table. "The guy's English wasn't that good. He knew what you looked like and where you lived and when you would get off shift. It was all typed out on a piece of paper."

A chill snaked up and down Austin's back. How would a gang member have that kind of info unless he had contact with someone on the inside? All border patrol and rangers were playing a game of who-can-you-trust. The pay really didn't compensate for the level of danger they encountered every day. Sometimes, when faced with mounting debts or sudden emergencies, agents or even rangers would justify selling bits of information to the money-laden cartels. "Do you have that piece of paper?" It might have fingerprints on it.

"I threw it away," Mark said.

Kylie shifted in her seat and brushed her hand over her auburn hair. The information must have alarmed her too.

"Were you the one taking shots at us while we were in the desert last night?" Austin leaned on the table and looked right at Mark, watching his body language.

"I don't know anything about that." Mark was still maintaining eye contact when he spoke, a sign he was telling the truth. "All I know is I got the call to take up my position and that you would be coming home shortly."

Mark must have been the back-up plan when the guy in the desert didn't succeed at his mission.

"Is there anything else you remember about the man who hired you?"

Mark's gaze rested on Kylie. "When he talked about you, I could tell he was really angry."

"Angry about her being a border patrol agent?"

"No, it seemed more personal than that."

Kylie jerked slightly in her seat. "But you didn't know there was a child involved. He didn't say anything about her."

"I wouldn't have taken the job if I had known there would be…that a child might be in the line of fire." Mark puckered his lips as though something had occurred to him, and then he shook his head.

Austin leaned on the table. "What did you just think of, Mark? Don't dismiss it. It might be important."

"My mind is so fuzzy." He cupped his hands on his head and squeezed, showing his teeth in frustration. "I just want my brain to work right again."

"Tell us what you remember even if you are not sure about it," Kylie said.

Mark let out a heavy breath. "Like I said, the guy's English wasn't very good. I thought he said something about getting revenge on his Valentine." Mark shook his head. "Like I said. It didn't make a lot of sense."

Kylie was visibly upset. All the color drained from her face.

"Mark, you've done really good here. We'll have the officer set you up with that program, and we'll figure out who this man was." Austin patted Mark's shoulder.

Kylie scooted her chair back, then burst to her feet. "Please excuse me."

She pushed past Austin and ran down the hallway. Austin hurried after her.

Sure she was going to be sick to her stomach, Kylie leaned over the first trash can she could find. The attempt on her life was personal, and it was because of her connection to Valentina. That scared her far more than knowing someone would take shots at her because she wore a border patrol uniform.

She felt a warm hand on her back. "You gonna be okay?" Just having Austin close calmed her.

She straightened up. Her stomach was still doing somersaults.

"I guess I'm just in shock that this really does have something to do with Valentina. Do you think it is more revenge for her being an informant? How did they find out Valentina and I were connected?"

Austin shook his head. "Inside information."

Ice froze in her veins. The ranger company "E" and border patrol shared intel connected to the cartel cases. It could be a ranger or it could be an agent leaking the information. "I didn't want to consider that possibility." Kylie collapsed into a chair. Her head was still spinning. "My schedule would have been easy enough to find out, but only my supervisor knew the identity of my informant. And he wouldn't have been involved in something like this."

"Somehow someone found out." Austin pulled a chair up beside her and laid a hand on her forearm. "I'm sure El Paso PD will give us a call if Mark comes up with an ID on the guy who hired him. Do you need to head back home?"

Kylie rose to her feet. "I have to be back out on patrol tonight. I can catch a nap while the sitter is with Mercedes." She walked briskly toward the exit doors. Austin kept pace with her.

Kylie found herself checking rooftops as she and Austin stepped out into the El Paso heat and headed toward the parking garage. It always felt strange to have Thanksgiving be just around the corner while the daytime temperatures hovered around seventy.

Austin was checking the rooftops, as well.

Her job involved a high degree of danger. She'd known that when she signed up for it. She'd seen firsthand how ruthless the drug cartels could be. But she'd never expected to be personally targeted. She felt vulnerable and exposed.

Austin stayed close to her, walking her to her car.

He lingered while she fumbled in her small purse for her keys.

"That was impressive in that interrogation room. The way you forgave Mark."

She stared into his blue eyes. "I meant it. I know interrogation is a lot of game playing to get a suspect to talk, but that wasn't what I was doing. I could see Mark wasn't a bad man. He showed remorse. He wants to change."

He stepped closer to her. His hand cupped her arm just

below her shoulder. The warmth of his touch seeped through her skin. “I know. I just hope that if the time ever comes for me to forgive like that, I will be able to do the same.”

The warm admiration in his gaze made her knees weak. The sudden rush of attraction caught her by surprise. She turned back toward her car and hit the key fob to unlock the door. She didn’t want Austin to see her flushed cheeks. She just wasn’t used to the Lone Wolf being so connecting. Once the heat in her face faded, she turned back to face him. She wanted to get to know him better…outside of work. “Maybe some Sunday you can scoot on up and sit by me in church.”

“I’d like that.” His voice smoldered. “Kylie, considering the threat against you, maybe I should follow you home.”

“Okay.” Feeling a charge of electricity over her skin, she swung the door open and got inside. She tried to remind herself that there could never be anything more than a friendship between her and Austin. Every time she opened the door to that hope, it got slammed in her face.

She pulled out and waited for him to get to his car. Her last glimpse of him was in the rearview mirror as he opened his car door.

Kylie left the parking garage and pulled out onto a busy street. Once she was away from downtown, traffic evened out. She clicked the blinker to turn into her neighborhood. She couldn’t see Austin’s car anywhere, but a dark blue car hung close to her bumper. Hadn’t that car been pulling out of the parking garage the same time she had?

Her heart skipped a beat. If she was being followed, she wasn’t about to lead them to her home and to Mercedes. If this was about her connection to Valentina, would they be so ruthless as to kill Valentina’s child as well, all for revenge? She wasn’t about to chance it.

Kylie took a sharp turn away from her neighborhood, but then started second-guessing the decision. The man who had paid for her hit already knew where she lived. Panic surged through her. What if they had already gotten to Mercedes? Kylie felt like she couldn't breathe. She checked the rearview mirror. No blue car and no Austin.

Maybe news that the hit was personal was just making her paranoid. She took another turn to redirect herself back to her apartment. The desire to be with Mercedes, to make sure she was safe, overwhelmed her.

The blue car appeared again, filling up her mirror and edging very close to her bumper. Heart racing, she accelerated. She didn't recognize the street she was on. Mentally, she tried to reroute herself. The street merged with a much busier one. Noonday traffic was in full force. The blue car tailed her closely.

She sped up, watching the needle tip to a dangerous speed as she wove in and out of traffic. She lost the blue car for a moment and then caught a glimpse of it two cars behind her.

She studied the signs up ahead. All she had to do was get to a safe, public place. The exit ramps were for dangerous neighborhoods. If she could get closer to the shopping district, she'd pull off.

The blue car was right behind her. She clicked her blinker to change lanes. The car tapped her bumper. She jolted forward in the seat but held on to the steering wheel.

Other cars seemed to be clearing away from them, switching lanes to not get in an accident. The car rammed her again. The steering wheel jerked in her hand. The back end of the car fishtailed. She saw the guardrail looming toward her as her car spun out of control.

The crush of metal grated on her ears. She felt her

body being jerked around. Her head hit a hard surface before her world went black.

Moments later, a tapping sound came from far away as though she were wearing earmuffs. Someone called her name.

When her eyes blinked open, she saw Austin pounding on her window. She was so shaken up it took her a moment to determine where the handle was for rolling down the window.

"Sorry I lost you in traffic." Austin reached in and pulled up on her door handle. "The door is smashed in. Can you push on it from the inside?"

Her traumatized brain was slow in processing his instructions, but she finally got the idea. She unclicked her seat belt and then pushed with both hands. Austin gripped the rim of the open window and pulled. The door came completely off its hinges.

Austin reached in to pull her out. As he gathered her into his arms, she caught a glimpse of the wreckage around her. Two other cars, neither of them the blue car, had been damaged in the accident. Smoke furled out of the bent hood of a car still in a traffic lane. The other car had slammed into the guardrail right next to hers.

She heard sirens in the distance. Austin placed his hand on her cheek. "You all right?"

She nodded even though her head felt lighter than air, and her legs wobbled beneath her. Maybe she wasn't all right. Black dots encroached around her vision. His strong arms encircled her. Right before her world went dark again, her only thought was that she needed to get to Mercedes…to make sure she was safe.

SIX

Austin felt a tightness in his chest that made it hard to breathe as he watched the ER doctor check out Kylie. The nurse had already bandaged a cut on her forearm.

Even hours after the accident, the color still hadn't returned to Kylie's cheeks. And the look in her eyes was wild.

The doctor, a woman with gray hair in a tight bun, leaned close to Kylie and shone a light in her left eye and then her right. "X-rays show no broken bones. Just some scrapes and bruises." She shut off the light and put it back in the pocket of her lab coat. "However, I do think you have sustained a mild concussion."

Kylie touched the bruise on her arm and then rested a hand on her forehead. "I guess I'm not going to work tonight."

The doctor shook her head. "The best thing for you is rest and no intense activity for at least twenty-four hours. After the first day, if you don't lose consciousness again, you'll be out of the woods for the bump to your head being more serious. It would be good if you had someone to stay with you...just in case."

Austin stepped toward her. "I can do that, stay with her."

Kylie sat up straighter on the exam table. "What about your work?" Her voice sounded a little frosty. Then again, he might be way off base. He'd never been any good at reading the signals women gave off.

"I'm due for some downtime, and we're not running any crucial operations tonight. Not until we can get some sort of strong lead on Garcia. Unless of course you had someone else in mind..."

Kylie shook her head. "Not anyone in law enforcement." She bit her lower lip. "If they come after me again, it would be good to have you around until I'm sure I'm recovered. All I know is I need to go get Mercedes. That's all I care about right now."

Austin took in a breath. At least she wanted his protection.

"I'll leave you two alone," said the doctor. "Stop at the checkout desk to pick up your paperwork."

Austin stepped toward Kylie. "You passed out for a moment." It had scared him more than he'd expected. In his line of work, he'd had plenty of people lose consciousness around him, but this was different.

The truth was he felt an attachment to Kylie he didn't understand. All the rangers had each other's backs. That was assumed. And if they were working joint task with border patrol, the same rule applied. But his desire to protect Kylie, to keep her safe, ran deeper than that. Maybe it was just because he admired her so much.

"Come on, I'll take you home to get that baby."

Kylie closed her eyes and tilted her head toward the ceiling. "Could you please call her by her name."

"Sorry," he said. He hadn't meant to hurt Kylie's feelings. He just didn't know how to act. Babies were as foreign to him as a trip to the moon.

Kylie jumped off the exam table. "My phone, my purse, everything got left in my car."

"I'm sure the traffic investigation unit will get those things back to you."

"Can I borrow your phone? I need to call Mrs. Espina and make sure Mercedes is okay."

He pulled his phone out of his back pocket and handed it to her. His fingers brushed over hers. A jolt of electricity raged through him at her touch. "I'll…um…deal… um, with your paperwork while you make the call."

He walked away shaking his head. Okay, so maybe it was more than just admiration that made him feel connected to Kylie. He was attracted to her. He could hear Kylie talking on the phone as he spoke in a hushed tone to the woman at the desk. The administrative clerk handed him two pieces of paper. She glanced at them. "It looks like Dr. Sanchez wants to do a follow-up appointment with her in a couple of days."

Austin nodded and turned to face Kylie.

She handed him his phone. "Mercedes is fine. Let's get going." She hurried toward the exit.

As they walked through the parking lot toward his car, he thought about the accident. "I think we can assume that the same guy who hired Mark Smith had something to do with that accident."

"Did they catch the driver?"

Austin shook his head. "He sped away from the accident. There was a lot of confusion."

"I'm glad you were following me." She planted her feet and looked directly at him. There it was again, that look that he couldn't quite decipher. All her features seemed to soften and her deep green eyes looked right through him. Was it appreciation between colleagues or something deeper?

"I wish I hadn't lost you in traffic," he said.

"You wouldn't have been able to prevent the accident." She touched his forearm lightly. "I'm just glad you were there to help me." Her voice fused with warmth, causing his heart to beat faster.

Okay, he liked her. He could admit that much, even if he knew he could never act on it.

They got into his car and Austin pulled out into the flow of traffic. "Kylie, I don't think you should stay at your place."

"I know. It doesn't feel safe. They know my work schedule. They know where I live. They knew I was going to be at police headquarters to question Mark." Her voice faltered as she laced her fingers together and rested them in her lap.

"I don't think my place would be smart, either. If they've figured out where you live, I'm sure they can find the addresses of the people you work with or anyone you're associated with."

"It needs to be a place where Mercedes can sleep," Kylie said. "She's adjusting too…to this new life without her mom."

Austin's phone rang. He didn't want to answer it while he was driving. "Can you get that?"

Kylie picked the phone up off the console where Austin had set it. "This is Kylie Perry. I'm answering on behalf of Austin Rivers." The conversation after that consisted of Kylie saying yes several times. She ended the conversation with a thank-you.

Kylie stared at the phone. Austin sensed that something had shifted for her.

"Everything okay?"

"That was El Paso PD."

He gripped the steering wheel. He glanced at her. She looked as though she'd been punched in the stomach. "Kylie?"

"They identified the man who hired Mark Smith by his tattoos. A snake on his neck and a scorpion on his hand."

"That's good." Austin cut his gaze at Kylie and then focused on the road. "So who is the guy?"

"The man's name is Miguel Ibarra." Her voice was flat, revealing no inflection at all.

Austin was confused. Why was Kylie shutting down? She seemed to be going into shock. "That's good, right? A step in the right direction. Can they link him back to Garcia?"

Kylie nodded. "He's in the system. Gang member. Low-level drug runner." Kylie stared through the windshield as though she was looking a million miles away.

"All of that sounds like progress. So what's wrong?"

She turned to face him. "Miguel Ibarra is Mercedes's father. Valentina told me. She said he was a bad man. She severed his parental rights."

Austin felt like the wind had been knocked out of him. He pressed on the gas, knowing that he could not drive fast enough to get to Mercedes and ease the fear that must be raging through Kylie.

Kylie watched the street names click by, appreciating that Austin must be feeling the same sense of urgency that had consumed her thoughts. Mercedes could be in danger. Would this man kill his own daughter or simply take her to satisfy his hurt pride? She wanted to believe that he would not harm his own flesh and blood, but she couldn't be sure.

Austin turned onto the street where she lived. He reached over and patted her leg. "We're almost there."

Something had shifted between them. He seemed more emotionally connected to her. Mentally, she kicked herself. It didn't matter. Austin saw Mercedes as some sort of encumbrance to her doing her job. If he couldn't accept that Mercedes was a part of her life, she could never be anything more to him but a trusted officer in the border war fight.

He pulled up to the curb, and she jumped out. She ran to her apartment door, expecting it to be open. The handle didn't budge. This was a safe neighborhood and it was daytime, Gloria normally didn't lock the door. Her stomach clenched as her heart pounded wildly.

Austin came up behind her.

She peered through the windows, not seeing Mrs. Espina or Mercedes. Maybe they were hiding just like Doris had hidden when they went to get Mercedes. Mrs. Espina might have locked the door because she had seen something threatening. "My key is back in my purse. I can't get into my own place."

Austin edged closer to her. "Try knocking."

Something about him standing so close, speaking with such authority eased her fears. She knocked several times. No answer.

"Maybe she locked the door and went somewhere else with the baby."

Why couldn't Austin call Mercedes by her name? It was like he wanted to distance himself from Kylie's new reality. "She sounded fine when I called her. That was only fifteen minutes ago when she was still at the apartment." Kylie reached for her phone. "I'll call her again."

Austin looked all around. "She couldn't have gone far. Let's check her place."

"Yes, she lives just across the courtyard, first floor." At least he was good at problem solving. Her fear over what might have happened to Mercedes made it hard to think straight. Only holding Mercedes and seeing her sweet face would ease Kylie's worried heart.

They ran across the courtyard. Kylie pounded on the door. Seconds ticked by. She knocked again. Her heart boomed against her rib cage as she pushed past the rising panic. "Give me your phone. I'm going to call her."

A voice floated down from above them. "Hello, Kylie?"

Kylie tilted her head. A woman of about Mrs. Espina's age stared down at her. She did not recognize her.

Kylie took a step back to have a clearer view of the woman. "Yes." She was a Hispanic woman with blond hair and a welcoming smile.

"I'm a friend of Gloria's. She and the baby are up here. We've been watching for you."

The tension in her muscles eased up. "I'll be right up." Kylie took the stairs two at a time.

Mrs. Espina's friend stood to one side so Kylie could enter the living room. Austin stepped in behind her.

Mrs. Espina rose to her feet. "The little one is all right. She's sleeping in the next room."

More than anything Kylie wanted to run and gather Mercedes into her arms.

"What happened? Why did you leave Kylie's place?" Austin, ever the practical one, was calm enough to ask questions.

"After what happened to Kylie the other day, I keep

a close watch out the window. I saw three men in the courtyard, looking around, up to no good, not men who live around here," Mrs. Espina said.

Kylie gathered the older woman into a hug. "You did the right thing."

Mercedes's plaintive cry was like a magnet to Kylie. She ran into the next room to get her daughter. The little girl lay on her stomach on a bed surrounded by pillows. Her cheeks were flushed from sleep and Mrs. Espina had put a strand of her dark hair in a fastener with a flower on it. The hair stood up straight on the top of her head like a sprig of parsley.

"There's my little sweetie."

Mercedes offered her a smile that had two pearl-like teeth in it. Kylie reached out and gathered the little bundle into her arms. Now she felt like she could take a breath after the scare she'd had.

Kylie bounced Mercedes and patted her back. "You look like your mama, you know that?" She drew the baby closer. "She was a good person. I know you miss her even if you don't understand all that is happening."

She stepped back out into the living room where Mrs. Espina's friend was handing Austin a steaming plate of something.

Austin grinned. "They're feeding me."

Mrs. Espina waved her hand in the air. "He too skinny."

The other woman pointed toward the kitchen while she looked at Kylie. "I have more. You could use some meat on your bones too. My name is Mary, by the way."

Austin dug into what looked like a delicious plate of pork stew in green salsa.

Kylie bounced Mercedes. Mexican spices floated in the air. "Maybe a small plate."

Mary bustled into the kitchen, and a moment later Kylie heard the microwave whirring.

Austin spoke after chewing a bite of food. "Mrs. Espina thinks we could stay the night at her church. There's a nursery there for the baby."

"I called pastor. He won't mind," Mrs. Espina said.

If suspicious men were skulking around the neighborhood, Kylie knew it wasn't safe to go back to her apartment. "That sounds like a temporary solution, but I think it's a good idea."

"I get the little one's things." Mrs. Espina stepped into the room where Mercedes had been sleeping and returned a moment later with the baby bag.

Kylie handed Mercedes over to Mrs. Espina so she could eat. Mrs. Espina swayed with Mercedes and then took a chair close to where Kylie was sitting. The little girl reached her arms toward Kylie and made a fussy noise.

"I'll be done in a minute, baby girl." Kylie spoke in a soothing tone and took a bite of food. It made her feel good that Mercedes was reaching for her. She could never replace Valentina, but that the baby had started to bond with her was a good sign. Maybe she could do this mom thing.

They ate, then gathered Mercedes and her things together. Mrs. Espina wrote down the address of the church. "Pastor lives next door. He'll make sure it's unlocked."

Kylie borrowed the key she'd given Mrs. Espina and swung by her place to grab a toothbrush, a change of clothes and to get Mercedes's car seat out of her car.

Austin helped her load the things in his car. He closed the trunk and stared at her intensely. "We agree this is a temporary solution, right?"

"It will work for tonight." She clenched her jaw. She knew what he was hinting at. He was going to bring up protective custody for Mercedes again. If Miguel Ibarra was trying to kidnap his daughter, it made sense. All the same, she questioned Austin's motives. It seemed as though he had no place for children in his world and didn't want to deal with her being a mom.

But what mattered here wasn't what Austin wanted or even what Kylie wanted, but rather what was best for Mercedes. Kylie wrestled with conflicting emotions. The little girl had been through so much trauma already. She'd lost her mother and was just starting to bond with Kylie. Interfering in that bond could damage Mercedes emotionally even more. What was the best thing to do?

A heaviness mixed with fear settled on Kylie as she fastened Mercedes in the back seat and brushed her fingers over the little one's soft cheek. "It's going to be all right, baby girl."

As she buckled herself into the passenger side seat, Kylie prayed she was telling Mercedes the truth.

SEVEN

The sky turned a dusky shade of gray as Austin drove through the city. The horizon glowed orange and pink. El Paso sunsets were some of the most beautiful in the world. It was already dark enough that the gigantic star on the side of the Franklin Mountains glowed.

The church was on the edge of the city, just past several subdivisions. He checked the rearview mirror several times to make sure they weren't followed. Finally, two adobe buildings surrounded by desert landscaping came into view. He pulled into the paved lot where only one other car was parked. The door of the smaller house opened, and a man came out. He greeted them with a wave. He was a young slim man, maybe in his late twenties. That must be the pastor.

Austin stopped the car and got out to talk to the pastor while Kylie unloaded Mercedes.

"I'm Pastor O'Conner." He held out his hand to Austin. The red hair and freckles made him look even younger. "It's all open for you."

"Thank you for letting us stay the night."

"Churches don't get much use during the week. Mrs. Espina vouched for you. I'm glad to be of help. I'll be right next door if you need anything." The pastor hurried back inside his little house.

Austin grabbed the two bags Kylie had brought with them. The evening light made her hair look even more coppery. He couldn't see the effect it had on her skin with the way she pressed her face close to the baby's.

Even hinting at how precarious this situation was had upset her. Why didn't she see that protective custody for the baby would be the best thing for both of them?

They found the church nursery and settled in. Austin checked all around the church as a precaution and to familiarize himself with the layout in case they were attacked.

They were far enough away from the subdivisions that he could hear if anyone pulled into the lot.

He returned to the nursery where Kylie had settled on the couch and was feeding Mercedes a bottle. "If I can get her to sleep, I'd like to rest a little myself."

"That sounds good. I'll keep watch and wake you after you've had a decent amount of sleep." Austin paced and examined the windows and walked through the church yet again, checking to make sure all the doors were secured. When he came back to the nursery, Kylie was rocking Mercedes, singing to her and looking into the little girl's eyes.

The scene tugged at his heart in a way he didn't understand. His mother must have taken care of him when he was a baby, but he had no memories of it. He wasn't sure how to respond to such tenderness between a mother and child.

The baby nodded off and Kylie laid her on her stomach in the crib. Kylie settled on the couch with her back to Austin.

"I'll take watch in a little while," she said in a sleepy voice.

Austin found a couple of baby blankets and placed them on Kylie.

Austin sat in the rocking chair as the sky grew dark outside. He watched mother and baby sleeping. Kylie was going to have to face reality sooner or later. Mercedes needed more protection than she could give.

Mercedes rolled over in her crib. Her eyes shot open and landed on Austin. She studied him. He was relieved to note that she didn't cry out. It was too soon for Kylie to be awakened. She needed sleep after all she'd been through.

Mercedes pulled herself up in the crib and continued to watch Austin. If the kid cried out, it would wake Kylie for sure. He stepped over to the crib and gingerly gathered Mercedes in his arms. He held her loosely. She seemed so fragile.

Her soft, dark hair brushed under his chin. She smelled like fresh-cut flowers and early mornings all rolled together. Gripping Austin's collar, the little girl drew back and continued to stare at the creature holding her.

Maybe if he walked with her, she'd stay quiet long enough to give Kylie a chance to sleep. Austin paced through the church until he came to the sanctuary. There was a banner behind the pulpit that said Give Thanks framed with gold and orange leaves. There were boxes with canned goods in them that were labeled Thanksgiving Food Drive.

Austin walked up and down the aisle, bouncing Mercedes like he'd seen Kylie doing. That bouncing thing must be something women instinctually knew to do. It felt awkward to him.

Mercedes reached up and put her fingers on his ear.

The touch was how he imagined it would feel to have butterfly wings brush over his skin—so soft he barely felt it.

He turned to look at her. "What are you doin'?" His voice was just above a whisper.

She made a sound and grinned at him, revealing two tiny teeth.

Her smile took his breath away.

"Mercedes," he said as his throat went tight. "Aren't you the charmer?"

He walked with her through the sanctuary and into a little side room that was used for storage. Speaking in a low soft voice, he named the things he saw. "Those are hymnals, that's a broken Christmas decoration, and that looks like a lost and found." It didn't seem to matter what he talked about just as long as he kept talking. She stared at him, fascinated. He grabbed what looked like a baby toy from the lost-and-found shelf, a plastic ring that rattled when he shook it.

He stepped back into the sanctuary. Mercedes glommed onto the toy and shook it. Then she threw it to the floor and laughed.

"What are you doing?" He chuckled and shook his head. Her laughter was infectious.

She laughed again.

He put her down, then picked up the toy and held it out toward her. She scooted toward him half crawling and half dragging herself toward where he perched on his knees. She plopped down beside him, shaking and twisting the toy and then throwing it again.

Fine, if this kept her entertained. He crawled across the carpet and grabbed the toy again. The game continued for at least fifteen minutes before the repetition of it became hard to take. Mercedes didn't seem to tire of it though.

He shook the toy hard and fast and then handed it to her. He sat at the edge of a pew and watched her put the toy down and crawl away. She glanced back at him. Then turned around and came back to where he sat. She held her arms up to him, a gesture that made him feel warm straight down to the marrow of his bones.

She trusted him.

He gathered her into his arms. She rested close to his chest and fingered the buttons on his shirt. As he sat there in the quiet church, he supposed there was no feeling as wonderful in the world as that moment.

Kylie rushed into the sanctuary. The look of concern on her face softened. "There you two are. I was afraid something had happened."

"Do you want to hold Mercedes?"

Kylie shook her head, her features glowing. "The two of you look very comfortable."

Austin alerted to the sound of a car rolling into the lot. He jumped to his feet and handed Mercedes over to Kylie. "Sounds like we've got company."

"Maybe it's someone coming to see the pastor." Agitation colored Kylie's words.

"Maybe." He hurried toward the foyer where he would have a better view of the parking lot. He crouched low. Kylie remained in the shadows with Mercedes.

The orange glow of headlights cut through the darkness, then were turned off. Three men got out of the car. They headed straight toward the church.

This wasn't a friendly call. He needed to get Kylie and the baby out of there and fast.

"This way." He ushered Kylie toward a room off to

the side of the sanctuary that opened up to the back of the church. “Get in there. The door locks from the inside and the outside door is still locked. I’m going to sneak out and bring my car around to the back. I’ll gun the engine. When you hear that sound, run out and jump in the car.”

He heard the men shaking the locked front door. It was just a matter of moments before they broke a window or shot open the door. There was no time to call the police.

Kylie slipped into the room. He heard the dead bolt click into place. He waited until the men gave up on the front door and stepped away to look for another entrance before he slipped out the front, easing the door shut behind him.

He saw the men in the shadows, heard them cursing and ordering each other around as they tried to find access inside. The guns in their hands glinted in the moonlight. The men disappeared around the corner of the church. Austin made a run for his car.

He climbed inside. Just before he turned the key in the ignition, he heard the sound of shattering glass. The men had broken into the church.

He had only minutes to get Kylie and Mercedes out of danger.

Heart pounding, Kylie held Mercedes and listened. She heard glass shattering. She drew her little girl closer.

How quickly things changed from safe to dangerous. Seeing Austin holding Mercedes had made her heart leap. His attitude toward Mercedes seemed softer. Austin had called Mercedes by her name. But then everything had gone wrong.

She heard crashing sounds. Doors slamming. The men were searching the church.

Mercedes fussed and wiggled.

Fear shot through Kylie. "You have to be quiet, little one."

The door rattled.

Kylie placed her hand gently over Mercedes's mouth, praying she wouldn't make a noise. She swayed back and forth, trying to soothe the baby.

The door shook some more. She heard shouting in Spanish. One man telling the other to come and see.

Kylie moved closer to the outside door, listening intently. She dared not step outside until she heard the signal. What if men had been positioned by all the exit doors? She and Mercedes would be easy targets. She prayed Austin would make it to his car unharmed.

The rattling of the door stopped.

Kylie took in a breath.

Mercedes cried out.

All Kylie's muscles went rigid. She said a prayer that the intruders hadn't heard Mercedes.

Something thudded against the door and then crashed against it a second time.

Kylie winced. Mercedes cried out again, and Kylie didn't bother to hush her. It was too late now. They'd been found.

The sound of a revving engine had her flinging the outside door open just as the men broke through.

Kylie bolted toward the car, holding Mercedes close. Austin had gotten out of the car and was reaching for Mercedes. Kylie handed off the baby just as a man grabbed her from behind.

She wheeled around and landed a punch to the man's throat that made him gasp for air. Another man came at her. "Get in," Austin yelled as he raced toward the driver's side door. The back door was open and Mercedes rested on the seat.

Kylie dove into the back seat of the car, gathering Mercedes into her arms and slamming the door shut as the second man came at them, pounding on Kylie's window and then hanging on to the car as Austin hit the gas.

Despite her fear, Kylie spoke to Mercedes in a soothing voice as she secured the baby in her car seat. "It's going to be all right. Everything will be okay." She stroked Mercedes's cheek. "That's my little girl."

Mercedes cried.

Austin pulled out onto the road, turning sharply.

Kylie slid on her seat. She positioned herself so she could get belted in as Austin gained speed. She saw no cars up ahead on the dark road. When she looked behind her, two glowing orange headlights told her the men who had attacked them at the church were pursuing them.

This was a lonely stretch of road. It would be too easy to run them off. Help could not get there fast enough.

Though her heart pounded away in her chest, Kylie smoothed Mercedes's hair and continued to try to reassure her. Whatever danger surrounded them, her most important job was to keep Mercedes safe and unafraid. Mercedes's crying subsided.

"I just realized what road we're on. Where it leads. I'm looking for a place to turn." Austin kept his eyes fixed on the road. "We've got to get back to civilization."

"I know this part of the desert." Kylie studied the landscape that appeared mostly in silhouette and shadow. If they turned around, they'd be headed straight back toward their pursuers. "There's nothing up ahead." *Only places where people die and nobody finds them for years.* The thought chilled her to the bone.

Austin passed her his phone. "Phone my supervisor, Thomas Vance. Let him know what's happening. See if we can get some help out here."

Her fingers trembled as she pressed numbers on Austin's phone. Thomas picked up on the first ring. She explained their position and what had happened.

"I'll get men out there as quickly as possible." Thomas paused for a moment as though taking in a breath. "But, Kylie, it won't be fast enough. I'm confident Austin can get you out of this."

Kylie clicked off the phone, trying to take in a deep breath. The pursuers' car had gained on them.

"Hold on," said Austin. He cranked the wheel. They lumbered over the bumpy terrain and then spun the car around. The other car sped past them.

Austin accelerated, kicking up gravel.

Kylie stroked Mercedes's arm and started to sing a lullaby, hoping her voice would not give away how afraid she was.

She glanced out the window. The other car changed directions but took a moment to start moving again.

Austin increased his speed. "If the little one wasn't with us, I'd try to find a way to catch these guys."

It warmed her heart that he expressed such a protective attitude toward Mercedes.

They sped past the church. Kylie vowed she would help the kind pastor pay to repair the damage caused by the intruders.

The car remained behind them, drawing closer, the glowing lights like the eyes of a monster. Kylie took in a breath that felt like it had nails in it. The car drew close enough that she could see the shadowed silhouettes of two heads in the front seat. Her pulse drummed in her ears as her hand curled into a fist at the thought of her baby being taken by those men.

She remembered Valentina saying the baby's father had wanted nothing to do with her once he found out she was pregnant. If Miguel Ibarra wanted Mercedes back it wasn't out of love, it was the result of wounded pride, and perhaps the desire for revenge.

Mercedes kicked her legs and uttered a noise to get Kylie's attention.

The other car was within arm's length of their car as the dark road stretched before them. Austin gripped the wheel, giving only a quick glance in the rearview mirror.

The lights of the subdivisions came into view. The pursuers' car fell back several yards.

A car whizzed past them going in the opposite direction. A moment later, Austin's phone rang.

Kylie answered the phone. "Hey, it's Colt Blackthorn," the man on the other end of the call said. "Did I just pass you?"

"We're headed back toward the city." She craned her neck. "The car with our attackers is still on our tail."

"Let me get turned around. I'll see if I can catch them or at least scare them off." He hung up abruptly.

"That was Colt," Kylie said.

Austin nodded as though he had totally expected his fellow ranger to show up.

The other car seemed to be hanging back more and more the closer they got to the residential area. Kylie saw a second set of headlights behind her and then the pursuers' car veered off the road altogether with Colt right behind them.

Austin slowed as they entered the subdivision. He drove without speaking until they were on a street that had several restaurants and gas stations. "I think we lost them for now." He pulled into the lot of an all-night café. "I don't know about you, but all the running and fighting makes me pretty hungry."

Austin was as cool as a cucumber. Just another day at the office for him.

"Yeah, guess I could use a bite too." When she stared down at Mercedes, the baby was fast asleep. At least she'd been able to calm Mercedes.

Austin hurried around to her side of the car. After she got out, he reached in and unclicked Mercedes's car seat. He lifted the seat with the sleeping baby very carefully. Though the light streaming from the café was dim, she thought she saw Austin smile at the sleeping Mercedes.

Austin went ahead of her, holding the car seat. Before she stepped into the restaurant, she glanced out at the cars streaming by on the road past businesses and flashing neon.

She didn't like putting Mercedes in so much danger. Maybe Austin was right about protective custody. Maybe she never should have thought she could be a mom in the first place. Despair settled in her chest like a rock.

She knew the time in the restaurant was only a short reprieve. The men would come after her and Mercedes again, maybe before the night was over.

EIGHT

Austin chose a table positioned so he could watch through the windows for any cars that pulled into the lot. At the very least, Colt had managed to chase the thugs away, but those three men had been able to find them at the church. They must have followed them from Kylie's place. He wasn't about to let his guard down.

He took a seat opposite Kylie, rested his face in his hands for a moment, and then stared out the window, taking note of each car in the parking lot.

Though he'd never let on, the last couple of hours had rattled Austin more than anything that had happened in his career. Keeping Mercedes and Kylie safe was starting to feel very personal.

Kylie glanced around at the Thanksgiving decorations. Each table had a ceramic turkey and a small cornucopia. "I keep forgetting that holiday is coming up."

Kylie picked up a menu from the side of the table close to the window.

He smiled at the sleeping baby as her lips moved in a sucking motion.

A glance at Kylie revealed a look of admiration or maybe astonishment. He could never read women very well, unless they were criminals about to jump him—that, he was good at. But the little nuances of emotion were always hard for him to figure out.

"Mercedes is cute when she sleeps." He ran his fingers through his blond hair.

"Thank you for using her name." Her voice did sound different, and she kept staring at him, her face all glowing. Just 'cause he said something nice about her kid?

He shrugged. Kylie better not be getting notions of them being anything more than friends. This baby needed a father, and he had zero qualifications for that job.

The waitress, a plump older woman with hair a shade of red that occurred nowhere in the natural world, came over holding a pad and pen. "What a cute baby. You two must be so proud."

"Yes, we are," Austin said, not seeing the need to explain to a stranger that they weren't a family.

A playful smile graced Kylie's face as she stared at the menu.

"Can I get you two anything to drink while you decide what you want to eat?"

"I'd like a cup of hot tea," said Kylie.

"Glass of milk," Austin said.

His phone rang. His supervisor.

"Rivers here."

"Glad you're breathing."

"Colt catch up with those guys?"

"No, but he scared them off." Thomas cleared his throat. "Listen, Austin, I can appreciate you wanting to help a fellow officer out. But it's clear Garcia's men are gunning for Kylie. She's a good agent. She can take care of herself, but let's think about protective custody for the kid until she's not a target anymore so you two can focus on the Garcia mission."

"I agree, but it's not my decision," Austin said with a glance at Kylie. Her protective instincts toward Mercedes were so strong. It would be hard to convince her to turn the baby over to strangers. He needed Kylie's help. She was the one agent he knew he could trust. The notion that someone on the inside was passing information to Garcia and his men still plagued him.

"See if you can talk her into it," Thomas said.

"Will do," said Austin. He ended the call.

The waitress brought them their drinks.

Kylie folded up the menu. "I'll have the burger and fries."

Austin hadn't even had a chance to look at his menu. "That sounds good."

Mercedes yawned in her sleep and turned her head sideways, nestling into the car seat. Austin felt a tightness in his chest he didn't understand. How could someone so little make him feel so turned inside out?

Kylie smoothed the lacy collar of Mercedes's onesie.

He couldn't put it off any longer. "Kylie, now that we know for sure you're being targeted, my boss thinks it would be a good idea for you to put Mercedes into protective custody."

She shot him a look that was filled with anguish. "I want to help get Garcia and Ibarra. I want to see this thing to the end. After we get him, I'm asking for more monitoring and desk assignments."

The news hit him hard. One way or another, he was going to see less of Kylie.

She touched the bottom of Mercedes's tiny foot. "I see now that she needs protection—more than I can give her." Her eyes glazed and she looked away. "She's been through so much already. I'm worried that separation would harm her long-term. What if something happened and I wasn't there? I'd never forgive myself."

Now he understood her turmoil. Austin reached out to touch her hand, but she pulled away.

"That's what you wanted anyway, right? To get the baby out of the way, so I could just be Kylie Perry, trusted border agent."

"No…well, maybe it was at first." He felt like a clumsy teenager. No matter what he said, it was going to be the wrong thing.

"You never liked the idea of me being a mom."

He knew she was going to dig her heels in. He shook his head…not sure what to say in the face of her anger.

"Well, now you get what you want. Strangers will be taking care of Mercedes and I'll go back to being your sidekick."

"No, that's not it. I want the two of you to be safe." He caught himself from saying the next thought that popped into his head…*because I care about both of you.*

"I don't want anything bad to happen to Mercedes, but there's no one who will take better care of her than me, who will love her more."

"No one is arguing about that, Kylie."

Kylie buried her face in her hands. "She has been through enough. She lost her mom. She doesn't need to be separated from me too."

The waitress set their plates of food in front of them. Her tone of voice indicated that she knew she'd intruded on a very emotional conversation. "Can I get you folks anything else?"

Austin answered without making eye contact. "No,

we're fine, thank you." It tore him up to see Kylie in such distress. "I know this is a hard decision."

She crossed her arms over her chest and looked off to one side. "I just don't know what to do."

"Kylie, I think the best place for you is to be with Mercedes and protected." He hated the idea of losing her help but this wasn't about him and his job.

Her expression brightened some. "Thank you. It might have to come to that."

He saw now how selfish he had been. "It's your life. I see what a difficult choice this is for you," Austin said. The salty aroma of the fries hit his nose. His stomach growled. "I do know what we need to do in the next twenty minutes. Dig in, little camper, I'm sure you're just as hungry as I am."

Kylie let out a laugh. "Little camper?" Kylie lifted her burger and took a big bite.

"It's something my parole officer used to say to me all the time," Austin said.

Kylie stopped chewing and studied him.

"Yes, it's true I wasn't always a fine upstanding citizen." He stared at his plate and then dared a nervous glance at her, not sure how she would take the news that he had been a juvenile delinquent.

Kylie set her burger down. "Well, that just makes you more interesting and less vanilla flavored, doesn't it?"

Her acceptance of his past lifted his mood. "I've always been a rocky road kind of guy myself." He was reminded again of how quickly she forgave the sniper who had taken a shot at her. Her capacity for generosity and understanding amazed him.

"I've always been a moose tracks girl myself."

"Moose tracks? That doesn't sound very appetizing." He stuck his tongue out.

"It's a Montana ice cream, caramel and tiny peanut butter cups in vanilla." She ate several French fries.

He bit into his burger, enjoying the rich, juicy flavor of the beef. They ate in silence for several minutes until their plates were nearly empty. Both of them were beyond exhausted. And Kylie probably hadn't fully recovered from the accident. But at least now with a full stomach, he felt like he could think straight. Kylie seemed to be perking up, as well.

"You know this problem would go away if Miguel Ibarra was behind bars," Kylie said. "Even if Garcia remains out of our grasp."

"Yes, all things point to Ibarra putting the hit on you and Valentina."

"But he's after me because he's angry that Valentina was my informant. Maybe he wants to steal Mercedes back, but it's not because he loves her. Valentina told me Mercedes's father wanted nothing to do with her. Getting to Mercedes is about possession and revenge."

"Revenge seems likely. I know how those kinds of guys think. It's all about not feeling disrespected. What Valentina did was the ultimate in betrayal." Though he kept the thought to himself, he was plagued by the idea that maybe Ibarra just wanted Mercedes dead along with Kylie. It didn't seem like Ibarra would have a sudden change in personality and want to act like a father.

Kylie rubbed her French fry in a slather of ketchup. "I know you're right. Protective custody is the best thing for Mercedes." Her voice faltered. "I can't protect her by myself like she needs to be protected."

It tore Austin up to see Kylie so distraught. "You're a good mom, Kylie. No one is saying you're not."

"Thank you for saying that. I'm struggling with a lot of doubt." The compliment seemed to bring Kylie around. She lifted her chin and took in a breath. "That's the way it has to be, then. We put Mercedes in protective custody. I appreciate the offer to go into custody with her, but I'd rather keep working the case directly. I want to help take Ibarra down. The sooner Ibarra is off the street, the sooner I can be a mom again."

"That sounds like a plan," Austin said.

Kylie rubbed her temple and then gazed over at the sleeping baby. "And then the two of us can get on with our lives."

The phrase "the two of us" felt like a stab to Austin's chest. Of course Kylie was seeing herself as raising Mercedes alone. Why, then, did it bother him so much?

Kylie watched the bank of monitors in the border patrol surveillance room. Cameras and ground sensors were set up at key locations in the desert where Mexicans were likely to try to cross the border. She studied each monitor.

Though it was her job tonight to be alert for any activity, she watched the screens looking for one man in particular, Miguel Ibarra. She'd memorized his photograph. The long dark hair usually drawn back into a ponytail, the snake tattoo on his neck and the scorpion on his hand made him easy enough to identify. The images on the screen were murky at best. She wouldn't be able to see the details of the tattoos tonight. But Ibarra was distinctive enough that she was certain she'd know him if she saw him.

Greg Gunn, a rookie border patrol agent, sat beside her, watching the screens, as well. "Quiet night, huh?"

The only other person in the room was an older agent. Tom Kineer rarely went out in the field now that he was less than a year away from retirement.

After the excitement she'd had the last couple days, she was grateful for a calm night and to be sitting in front of the monitors where Ibarra was less likely to get at her.

"Yes." She looked at the screens again. "Not much going on." Mercedes was safe in protective custody. A husband-and-wife police officer team was watching her. Kylie had met George and Julie before handing Mercedes over to them. They seemed like good cops who would take solid care of Mercedes. That knowledge did nothing for the hole Kylie felt in her heart.

"I get antsy just sitting here," said Greg, "but Lena likes it when I'm not out in the field." Greg's face lit up and his voice brightened when he talked about his fiancée.

"How are the wedding plans with Lena going?"

Greg rolled his eyes toward the ceiling. "Lots of girl stuff. I just show up when requested."

Tom laughed. "I remember those days. My wife and I will be celebrating our fortieth soon."

Kylie sighed. Greg's description was probably how most men saw wedding preparations.

"Lena wants a big fancy shindig. Money just flies out of our pockets. But that's what we're doing," Greg said.

"What the bride wants, the bride gets," said Tom.

Ever since she'd signed up to be a border patrol agent, Kylie had assumed she would remain single. Her job didn't exactly make her look like good wife material. No one likes to kiss his wife goodbye and then wonder if she will come home alive. Now that she had become Mercedes's guardian, she probably looked even less eligible. It took a special man to accept a ready-made family.

Greg leaned a little closer to the screen. "Looks like the mobile camera has picked up something."

Kylie stared at the screen. At first, she saw only shadows. The longer she studied, the more readily she was able to discern the staggered movements of several people as they snuck from one bush to the next.

"None of those are your man Ibarra, huh?"

Kylie shook her head. She could discern one male—young, judging from the way he moved. The other two people were female. "Aren't the rangers running some sort of operation close to that sector tonight?"

"Yeah, Colt said something about that. They got word that one of Garcia's men might be moving some product," Greg said. "They're going to try to take him in and see if they can get him to flip."

Austin was probably out there too. She missed the action, and she missed working with him, but knew she was safer watching monitors.

The two women and the man sneaking through the brush were probably the mules, carrying the product to a drop-off point.

Tom ran his hands through his white hair. He stopped abruptly and then stood up from his chair. "Wait a second."

He put his finger on the screen. "There are more of them there." He pushed the rewind button and froze it. "There."

Kylie saw it then. Men hidden behind bushes and in the shadows. "It's some sort of setup, an ambush." Kylie pushed her chair back. She picked up the phone. "Is there a way to communicate with the rangers?"

"Not without giving away their position and risking their lives," Greg said. "It's radio silence tonight. They're only talking to each other."

"Then I'm going out there." She grabbed her coat. "It's ten minutes away."

"Kylie, the best thing for you to do is to stay put." Greg patted her chair.

Tom kept his eyes on the screen. "He's right. Your assignment tonight is to watch the monitors and send border patrol agents where they need to be."

"Don't you think I'm worried too? Colt is going to be best man at my wedding. The rangers can handle themselves," Greg reassured.

"You've got a bunch of other sectors that need your attention." Tom tilted his head toward the monitors. "And a bunch of other agents who are counting on you to be their eyes."

Agitated, Kylie sat back down in her chair. The men were right, but that didn't make staying there any easier. When she looked at the screen, the men they'd spotted were no longer visible in the frame.

"Isn't that camera run by remote control? Can't we get it back on those guys so we at least have footage that could be used in court in case something does go down tonight?"

Tom pushed buttons on the console.

Though the picture was bumpy, she watched the camera track along at high speed until she recognized the terrain where the rangers were hiding out. Now she didn't see anything. No movement at all. Her thoughts reeled as tension knotted the muscles in the back of her neck.

Had some disaster taken place in the moments that camera wasn't on them? She didn't see any lifeless bodies anywhere.

Greg placed his hand on her shoulder. "We have to pay attention to all of the border."

She pulled her eyes away from the one camera that might tell her if Austin was okay or not. The night seemed to drag on. A little activity by the river required them to dispatch agents but otherwise things were quiet.

Her eyes kept returning to the screen where Austin and the other rangers were probably still hiding out. Her stomach twisted every time she looked at that monitor.

Not only did she not like sitting in this chair, she didn't like being away from Austin. They had worked so closely for the last few days. When she wasn't with him it was like she lost a part of herself. She wasn't sure she liked that feeling.

Greg said, "There's been no activity in that sector for over an hour. That mobile camera needs to cover as much desert as possible. Let's get it moving."

Kylie knew she couldn't object. The mobile camera scanned the desert at a very slow rate. She watched the enthralling edge-of-your-seat footage of brush and cacti and the occasional nocturnal animal with its glowing red eyes.

She saw flashes in her peripheral vision. Her eyes fixated on the screen to her left. More flashes. "Gunfire."

Tom clicked the keys on his computer. "That's about a mile away from where the rangers were positioned."

"That doesn't mean it's them," said Greg.

"It doesn't mean it's *not* them, either." She watched the screen. Her throat went tight with panic. She saw shadows, men on the move, maybe? More gunfire caused quick flashes. It was hard to discern who was a ranger and who was a criminal. The rangers wouldn't be in uniform for an operation like this.

She felt utterly and completely helpless.

A man ran by in the corner of the screen. She took in a breath as ice seemed to freeze in her veins. She recognized Austin's distinctive gait. "It *is* them."

The man she thought was Austin fell to the ground, out of sight. Had he been shot?

Almost as quickly as it had erupted, the area went silent again. She saw brush shaking, more shadows, but no more gunfire. The picture on the screen was hardly high-definition, but it appeared that all activity had died down.

Kylie watched the screen in agony. Had the men gotten out okay? Was Austin even alive?

NINE

Austin's feet pounded the hard desert ground as he spotted some old buildings up ahead. He'd taken a risk separating from Brent and Colt to chase a suspect. The urgency he felt in capturing someone who knew what Garcia was up to drove him to run.

Brent and Colt would deal with the other suspects. At first, they'd seen only two women and a man. But three other men had been hiding out waiting, probably put there to protect the mules carrying the product. Or perhaps the rangers had been set up for an ambush.

Austin drew nearer to the buildings. He slowed, watching for signs of movement. The larger building had been a gas station at one time. There was a second building that looked like it might have been a house. The road had been paved at one point but now was broken up and overgrown with plants.

He edged toward the larger building, drawing his weapon. A rusty car with the doors and tires missing stood outside. He peered into the vehicle, not seeing anything. Noise emanated from inside the building. Wind caused a dilapidated metal sign, indicating that people could get gas and food, to creak.

The noise inside could have been the wind, as well. Or it could be one of Garcia's men.

He stepped toward the gaping door.

This night had felt off from the start. And not just because he wasn't working with Kylie.

Austin peered inside the building, seeing a mess of rubble, broken display cases and shelving. There were a hundred places the suspect could be hiding. He focused on the interior, section by section, as his own heartbeat drummed in his ears.

He moved deeper into the building. There was a second room behind a dusty counter. Austin moved sideways to clear the area behind the counter. Nothing. He kicked the door in and pressed against the wall expecting gunfire—instead, he found more shelving, canned goods and a table with three legs.

He turned to exit and a man jumped on top of his back. The goon bit down into Austin's shoulder and then tore the night vision goggles off his head. Austin spun around and landed several blows. The man dove at him again, this time tearing away his radio. Austin fought back, hitting him over and over.

Gunfire came from outside the building through a broken window. Another shooter. Austin ducked to the floor and scrambled after the first suspect who was headed for the front door.

More shots were fired at Austin as he exited the building. Austin returned fire. The man who had fought him inside rammed into him again, knocking him to the ground and causing the gun to fly out of his hand.

More shots were fired around Austin as he struggled to get the first suspect under control. The man dug his teeth into Austin's forearm. Pain shot all the way up his arm. This guy really liked biting.

Austin landed a hit to the man's face and then to his stomach. The man curled up to protect himself from more blows. Austin scrambled to his feet. He searched the ground for his gun but found nothing.

More shots rang in his ears. Austin sought cover inside the building. He picked up a piece of wood to use as a weapon.

Silence fell all around him like a shroud. He pressed against the wall. The gunfire was from close by. Judging from the sound, the shooter was using a handgun.

The man he'd fought with outside, the biter, groaned and crawled toward the shelter of the defunct car. That didn't mean he wouldn't recover and come after Austin again.

Two against one, and he was without a radio or a gun.

Austin breathed in a prayer for protection as he strategized. Running away was not an option. He needed to stand his ground. One way or another, he was going to take in one of these guys for questioning. He didn't want this night to be a waste.

He slumped down to the floor and raised his head so he could see above the windowsill. The shooter had to be fairly close. This part of the desert provided only a few places he could be hiding.

He peered inside the car. The first man, the biter, was gone. The building creaked as a gust of wind shot across the flat terrain. Metal bent by the wind made an eerie noise that sounded almost like a scream.

Austin settled in. The goons clearly were not leaving until he was dead. He would wait them out until their defenses were down or until Brent and Colt could get here. Or…he could come up with an offensive plan.

His shoulder and his arm stung where the first suspect had bit him. What a dirty tactic. He studied the area by the old car where he must have dropped his gun.

The night vision goggles were across the room, and could easily have been damaged when they were thrown on the floor. He dared not risk giving away his position by crawling around chasing after something that might be inoperable.

He searched for his gun. The moonlight caught no glint of metal in the dust. He wasn't sure where the biter had gone. What if the biter had found Austin's gun?

The seconds ticked by.

Austin had a thought. If the shooter was low on ammo, why not make him use it up? Making himself a target would be risky, but each shot would give the man's position away.

It was worth a try. Austin burst out of the gas station and ran toward the other building. His heart raced as he willed his feet to move faster. A single shot was fired close to his leg. Austin ran into what used to be someone's home.

A shredded curtain blew in the wind. A mattress lay in the corner of the room. He heard rustling noises that were probably mice scrambling for cover.

He realized now his foolishness in not working with his team. He had a rabid sense of justice when it came to getting the drug runners but in this particular case, something else was driving him even more. This war had become more personal to him. Innocents like Mercedes were caught up in it.

He never liked it when bad things happened to kids. He identified too closely with them because of his own abusive childhood. Thinking of that little girl, seeing

Kylie so tortured over the choices she had to make, took his need to put as many of these men in jail as he could to a whole new level.

The one shot had allowed him to pinpoint where the first shooter was. Smart snipers knew to shoot and move, shoot and move. This guy wasn't the greatest shot. Maybe he didn't use sniper tactics.

Austin made his way to the back of the house where two old cars, a Jeep and a truck rusted away. He slipped around the side. Once he was back on the front side of the house, he'd be exposed as he ran toward the first bush. The unknowns here were where the biter had gone and if he'd found Austin's gun.

Austin burst up and ran toward the first cluster of brush. His feet pounded the earth; his whole body was tensed, ready for a fight. Still no shots.

As he drew near the bush, he saw shadows and heard footsteps moving away from him. The shooter was on the run. Austin willed his legs to pump faster. In the dark, he caught flashes of a light-colored hoodie.

Austin leaped through the air and landed on the back of the running man. The impact as they hit the ground jolted him to life. Adrenaline raged through him like wildfire.

The two men wrestled, alternating who was on top. Austin nailed him with a hit to his face that seemed to stun him enough to give Austin the advantage.

"Roll over on your stomach. You're under arrest."

"For what? I'm an American citizen."

"Shooting at a police officer is a crime no matter where you're from." He cuffed the man. "And I think that we probably have enough evidence to link you to the drug run we interrupted."

"Oh, give me a break. I was out enjoying the desert evening. You assaulted me."

Austin rolled his eyes. Great, he'd just arrested a closet lawyer. "I'm not the one who sorts that out. My job is to take you in. Now get up on your feet."

He heard a clicking sound off to the side and then a commanding voice. "I don't think so, my friend."

Though he was shrouded in shadows, the biter aimed a gun, Austin's gun, right at Austin's head.

The man with the gun grinned sadistically. "I fear that it is over for you, amigo. Lights out."

Kylie scanned the dark terrain as she sat behind the wheel of the border patrol SUV. Against orders, she'd left the station and gone to search for Austin. She spotted two buildings and an old road up ahead. She pressed the accelerator.

She'd caught up with Colt and Brent who were also searching for their friend. His radio had gone black ten minutes ago. The news had knocked the breath out of her.

Kylie clicked off her headlights as she approached the dilapidated structures. The buildings would be a good place for a fugitive to hide. She killed the engine and slipped out of her vehicle. As she approached the buildings from the back, she saw a rusty Jeep and truck.

Kylie cleared both vehicles as possible hiding places and then slipped inside what appeared to be an abandoned house. Careful to keep her back to a wall to avoid an ambush, she checked the two main rooms.

Gunfire jolted her attention to outside the house. Heart pounding, she raced outside. She couldn't see anything, but she heard the sound of men wrestling, of blows being struck.

She ran toward the noise, aiming her gun at the moving shadows. "Border patrol. Put your hands up."

She heard footsteps pounding, at least one man getting away.

"Kylie."

Austin's voice was a welcome sound. She ran toward where he was sitting on the ground.

Out of breath, he paused between each word. "Two of them." He pointed each hand in a different direction. "You take that one." He pointed to the east and pushed himself to his feet, wobbling a bit. "He'll be slowed down. He's in cuffs."

She took off running, knowing that Austin would chase the other fugitive. She heard the culprit before she saw him. He stumbled and fell to the ground, releasing a string of curses.

She caught up to him, reached down and pulled him to his feet. She led him back through the brush to her SUV. Once he was secure in the back seat, she shone a flashlight on him. Not Ibarra. Of course it wouldn't be that easy.

Austin returned, out of breath. "I lost the other one."

"We've got this one to question," she said.

Austin turned from side to side and then ran his fingers through his hair. "Thanks for coming for me. I could hug you for that."

His comment caught her off guard. "We'll save the warm fuzzy moment for later." Maybe a hug from Austin wouldn't be a bad thing. She shone her flashlight on him. "You're bleeding."

He glanced at his shoulder and his forearm. "The one that got away likes to bite."

"Weird. Let me fix that up for you." She circled

around the car and pulled her first aid kit out from underneath the passenger seat. When she looked up, the suspect in cuffs glared at her. He sneered at her and made a lewd comment in Spanish.

"I'm not the one in handcuffs," she said.

She opened up the hatch on the SUV so Austin could sit.

"I was stupid tonight," he said. "I ran off without Colt and Brent to back me up."

She placed her hand underneath his forearm, wiped away the dried blood and applied the disinfectant. "That makes two of us. I'm supposed to be watching the monitors."

His skin was warm to the touch. She bent close enough to see the bite marks. Close enough to feel his body heat and hear his breathing.

He reached out and touched her forearm with his uninjured hand. "Thanks."

The word seemed to echo in her head, which felt like it was filled with helium. "It's what we do, right?" She made momentary eye contact as invisible heat sparked between them. More than anything, she wanted him to lean close, to kiss her.

His hand brushed over her cheek.

Letting go of his forearm, she grabbed the bandage from the kit and tore the package open. Feeling the weight of his gaze on her electrified her skin and made her heart pound.

What was happening to her? She shook free of the moment and handed him the bandage. "You can put that on yourself."

Touching Austin Rivers, being so close to him, had loosened the lid on a Pandora's box of out-of-control emotions. She wasn't sure if she liked that or not.

Feeling the heat between them falling away, she scooted the first aid kit toward him. "You can get your shoulder. I want to talk to this suspect."

"Sure." He glanced at her and then looked away.

Had he felt the same spark that had ignited her senses?

Kylie grabbed her Toughbook computer and pressed the power button.

"I'm an American citizen," said the suspect.

"That's not a get-out-of-jail-free card. You were in the vicinity of where drugs were being trafficked." She nodded toward Austin. "And I suspect he has a few charges he could add to that."

She clicked through her computer until Miguel Ibarra's photograph came up. "Do you know this man?"

Kylie watched the man's reaction to the photo. Even in the dim light, she caught a flash of recognition.

"What if I do?" The man drew his mouth into a tight hard line.

Anger surged through her. The safety of a little girl depended on her putting Ibarra behind bars. The nerve of this man to toy with her. His sheer arrogance caused the muscles in the back of her neck to knot up.

She swallowed her ire and spoke in a calm voice. "Tell me what you know about him and your life will get easier."

The man lifted his chin slightly. "How much easier?"

Her muscles tensed with rage as she pressed her teeth together. "Tell me what you know about him."

"Ooh, somebody is getting upset." The man grinned, looking maliciously delighted.

Kylie's grip on the computer tightened. She set the computer down and leaned in close to the suspect. "Right now, I want to shoot you." She wasn't lying. All she could think about was the way this man was toying with the welfare of her little girl.

The man drew his head back, clearly surprised and more than a little afraid, but his words still held a note of arrogance. “Police brutality.”

“Tell her what she wants to know.” Austin stood behind her. “We’re not making any deals with you. What you’re trying to avoid right now is the severest sentence we can get a judge to give you.”

Kylie wanted to applaud Austin. The ice-cold delivery of his words made his threat seem very real.

The man licked his lips as though he were contemplating his options. “He stays off and on with a guy named Limey Pete over on Mesa Verde Street.”

“That wasn’t that hard, was it?” Her spirits soared. They had a solid lead on tracking down Miguel Ibarra and ending her personal nightmare.

Austin took a step back. “Looks like we have company.”

He indicated the headlight off in the distance. Kylie stepped out away from her car and watched. Her hand hovered over her gun. She relaxed when she saw the familiar ranger insignia on the side of the SUV.

“I know we have a lot to answer for over the choices we made tonight. But all I want to do is get over to Mesa Verde Street as fast as possible,” she said.

“My thoughts exactly,” said Austin.

TEN

It took Austin only one phone call to the local police to find out that Limey Pete, aka Peter Sullivan, was a transplanted British man who had been busted for selling pot. The Englishman also had some assault charges pending, indicating that he was a potentially dangerous and violent man.

His last known address was indeed on Mesa Verde Street where the stucco-style homes were built into the side of a hill. Kylie and Austin set up surveillance outside his house in an unmarked vehicle.

Though surveillance had to be the most tedious part of his job, he was glad to be working with Kylie again.

Kylie sipped her coffee and stared out at the housing complex. It was early morning and neither of them had had any sleep.

Austin massaged the back of his neck. Squeezed his eyes open and shut. Sleep would be nice, but it wasn't his priority right now. He wanted to see this thing to the end, to give Kylie peace of mind and reunite her with Mercedes.

Children emerged from the buildings, making their way down the winding paths that surrounded the houses to play in the street down below. A smile graced Kylie's face as children riding skateboards held her attention. Though Kylie had to be as exhausted as him, there was still such elegance to her. The way she carried herself reminded him of a ballet dancer or maybe a swan on the water. This job required strength and stamina, but Kylie brought a feminine grace to it that he was coming to admire.

One of the boys on the skateboard hugged the other after recovering from a fall. "They're cute, aren't they?" Austin asked.

"Yes." Her eyes darted back up toward Limey Pete's house where so far there had been no activity.

"Not as cute as Mercedes though," he said.

She turned to face him; the brightness in her eyes made Austin think of warm sunshine. "Thank you for saying that. I wasn't sure how you felt about her."

He flushed from her staring at him, and he was reminded of her touch when she'd cleaned his bite wound. A charge of electricity shot through him at the memory of her fingers warming his skin. "I like her all right." The short time he had had with the baby in the church had caused a shift for him. He'd always felt awkward around babies. Something about Mercedes's rich brown eyes so filled with trust unlocked the affection inside of him.

Kylie stared through the windshield again, her gaze darting along the street and up the hillside. "That makes me feel good 'cause I'm falling in love with that little girl. I can't wait until she is officially my daughter."

He took a sip of his coffee and studied the hillside. His last mug shot showed Limey Pete with distinct bleach-blond hair, but it could have changed. The rap sheet said he was a tall thin man.

He wasn't sure what Kylie meant by her comment.

It seemed to be important to her that he like Mercedes. That's how moms were, he supposed. Truthfully, his feelings ran deeper than just liking the little girl. Mercedes had charmed her way into his heart.

Maybe someday down the road Kylie would meet a man who could be a good father to Mercedes, the kind of father she deserved. Despite the attraction he'd felt for Kylie out in the desert, he knew he wasn't the right man for that job.

Kylie lifted her chin. "Do you suppose those kids would be able to tell us if they've seen Ibarra around here? I don't want to waste the whole day here only to find out this trail has gone cold."

"Kids are good ones to ask. They notice a lot and they don't necessarily tell adults who they talked to."

"I'll give it a shot." Kylie clicked open her door. "They are more likely to talk to me than you."

"I agree," said Austin. "That's where working with a female border agent can come in handy."

"Thank you for seeing that as an asset." Kylie offered him a smile that warmed him to the marrow. "It's not always easy being a woman in this job."

He watched her cross the street and approach the children. She pointed up at the house where Limey Pete lived. Both boys nodded and pointed and a third older boy joined them. Progress, maybe?

He diverted his attention to the hillside and the other houses. A woman at the bottom of the development stepped out and hurried toward the bus stop up the street. He saw movement a little farther up the hill. The door on a balcony on the house next to Limey Pete's opened and a man stepped out holding a bottle.

Hispanic. Long ponytail. Austin's heart skipped a beat

as he grabbed his binoculars for a closer look. The man took a swig from the bottle.

Kylie continued to converse with the children. One of the boys stepped on his skateboard and pushed past her, flipping the skateboard with his feet and catching it. Kylie applauded. The more the kids trusted her, the more information they'd be likely to give her.

He brought the binoculars into focus. The man was wearing a shirt with a collar. Austin couldn't tell if he had a tattoo on his neck or not.

The man peered down the hill. For a moment, his gaze fixated on Kylie, and then he disappeared inside.

Austin surveyed the activity in the rest of the housing development and on the street. Still no sign that anyone was even home at Limey Pete's. At least five minutes ticked by. Another child, a girl of about seven or eight, joined the skateboarders and talked to Kylie.

The man from the balcony reappeared as the house's front door opened, and he stepped out and headed down the hill as though on a mission.

Austin's gut twisted tight. Even without a positive ID, his hackles had gone up. He pushed open the door and raced across the street to get to Kylie before the man did.

The man turned the corner. Kylie's back was to him as she spoke with the children.

Austin was halfway across the street when the children scattered right as the man came up to Kylie. Her back stiffened as he pressed close to her. He must have drawn a gun on her. The man pulled her gun out of her waistband and tossed it aside.

Austin's instinct to protect revved into overdrive as his heart pounded against his rib cage. He drew his gun while still running across the street.

The man, who was probably Miguel Ibarra, must have heard Austin's approach and swung Kylie around to face Austin, using her as a shield. He couldn't shoot Ibarra without risking Kylie's life.

A car zoomed up to the curb, its brakes squealing as it came to a stop. The man with the gun pushed Kylie into the back seat and got in beside her. The car sped away.

Austin's last glimpse of Kylie was through the back window as the man put the gun to her head.

As cold metal pressed against Kylie's temple, she stared down at the scorpion tattoo on the man's hand. Her heart squeezed tight with fear. This was Miguel Ibarra.

Ibarra shouted orders at the driver. "We've got to get her out of town. Away from witnesses."

Her hair had come loose from the ponytail in the struggle and hung in front of her face. She lifted her head as houses and then pawnshops, casinos and convenience stores clipped by. As they reached the outskirts of town, the businesses grew farther apart and became warehouses and used car lots.

Sweat trickled down the back of her neck as she took in a shallow breath.

"Why are you doing this?"

Ibarra pressed the gun harder into her temple. "No one disrespects me like you and Valentina and lives." Ibarra made a spitting sound.

"She only wanted a better life for herself and her baby, *your* baby." Her life was on the line. Was it possible Ibarra had any fatherly instinct at all that she could appeal to? "I'll take good care of Mercedes."

"My child raised by a border agent." Ibarra squeezed

Kylie's upper arm. "I don't think so. Valentina showed no respect. I had to kill her."

Though she had suspected Ibarra of killing Valentina all along, the confession still sent shock waves through her. Ibarra's thinking was so twisted. Everything was somehow an attack on his manhood.

The car sped up as they got to the edge of the city. She could see another housing development up ahead. But the driver turned onto a side road that would take them deeper into the desert.

The car slowed some on the dirt road. Kylie's mind raced, trying to come up with a way to escape or to break down Ibarra's defenses.

"Please, someone needs to take care of Mercedes. I will love her and take care of her. If you kill me, who will take care of her?"

"You need to die and so does that baby." Ibarra's voice was as cold as ice.

Kylie's mind and body slipped into a sort of fear-induced paralysis. She couldn't fathom the evil of a man who wanted his own child dead, all because he felt like he'd been dishonored. Her hope that maybe Ibarra just wanted to take Mercedes to raise himself was gone. The man had a heart as black as night.

The car hit a bumpy patch on the makeshift road and caught air. The jolt was enough to bring her back to reality. Right now, she needed to escape or get Ibarra's weapon away from him.

The driver of the car showed no sign of slowing down.

Kylie slumped even more to make Ibarra think she was weakening, giving up. He let up on the pressure to her temple, resting the gun close to his side and pointing it at her.

YOUR PARTICIPATION IS REQUESTED!

Dear Reader,

Since you are a lover of our books – we would like to get to know you!

Inside you will find a short Reader's Survey. Sharing your answers with us will help our editorial staff understand who you are and what activities you enjoy.

To thank you for your participation, we would like to send you up to 4 books and 2 gifts – **ABSOLUTELY FREE!**

Enjoy your gifts with our appreciation,

Pam Powers

SEE INSIDE FOR READER'S SURVEY

YOUR READER'S SURVEY "THANK YOU" FREE GIFTS INCLUDE:

▶ 2 lovely surprise gifts ▶ Up to 4 FREE books

PLEASE FILL IN THE CIRCLES COMPLETELY TO RESPOND

1) What type of fiction books do you enjoy reading? (Check all that apply)
❍ Suspense/Thrillers ❍ Action/Adventure ❍ Modern-day Romances
❍ Historical Romance ❍ Humor ❍ Paranormal Romance

2) What attracted you most to the last fiction book you purchased on impulse?
❍ The Title ❍ The Cover ❍ The Author ❍ The Story

3) What is usually the greatest influencer when you plan to buy a book?
❍ Advertising ❍ Referral ❍ Book Review

4) How often do you access the internet?
❍ Daily ❍ Weekly ❍ Monthly ❍ Rarely or never

YES! I have completed the Reader's Survey. Please send me 2 FREE books and 2 FREE gifts (gifts are worth about $10 retail) from each series selected below. I understand that I am under no obligation to purchase any books, as explained on the back of this card.

Select the series you prefer (check one or both):

❑ **Love Inspired® Romance Larger-Print** (122/322 IDL GMRJ)

❑ **Love Inspired® Suspense Larger-Print** (107/307 IDL GMRJ)

❑ **Try Both** (122/322/107/307 IDL GLYV)

FIRST NAME LAST NAME

ADDRESS

APT.# CITY

STATE/PROV. ZIP/POSTAL CODE

Offer limited to one per household and not applicable to series that subscriber is currently receiving.

She lifted her head slightly. Ibarra grinned at her, revealing metal front teeth. "You're pretty," he said.

A rage like she had never known flooded through her, though she was determined to hide it from this man. His comment had been an attempt to get an emotional reaction from her, be it anger or fear. She couldn't control this situation, but she could maintain control of herself.

Kylie took in a breath and pushed past the terror that had invaded every bone in her body.

The car hit another bump, making Ibarra look away from her to glance at the road ahead of them.

Kylie took advantage of the momentary distraction and lunged for the gun. Ibarra lifted it in the air. The gun went off. She grabbed for it. The gun fired a second time as the two of them struggled in the back seat.

The car swerved wildly. The driver had been hit by the stray bullet. The horn sounded as his head impacted with the steering wheel. The car rammed into a cactus and jolted to a stop. Kylie and Ibarra, neither of whom had seat belts on, were flung around in the back seat.

Kylie hit her shoulder against the backside of the front seat. The front windshield was cracked.

Ibarra raised his head, probably disoriented from the impact of the crash. The noise of the horn continued to split through the desert quiet.

Her gaze darted around, searching for the gun. She didn't see it anywhere. She made a split-second decision to run.

Still battered and shaking from the crash, she pushed open the door. Her feet hit the ground, and she sprinted, gaining momentum. A shot sounded behind her, proving that Ibarra had found the gun. There was nothing she could do but keep running. The flat desert terrain provided no place for cover.

She glanced over her shoulder. Ibarra had pulled the driver out from behind the steering wheel and was crawling into the driver's seat himself.

She glanced in the other direction where a cloud of dust was being stirred up by a car. She ran toward that vehicle. As she drew close, she saw that it was the unmarked car she and Austin had been using. The car stopped. Austin got out and sprinted toward her.

She fell into his arms.

ELEVEN

Austin felt like he could breathe again now that he was holding Kylie and she was safe. Watching her be abducted, fearing that he would not get to her in time had been one of the most helpless feelings he'd ever experienced.

He drew her close as she buried her head against his chest.

He couldn't quite make out what she was saying. She was so distraught.

"Kylie, I can't understand you."

She took in a breath, slowed down and repeated herself. "He wants to kill the baby too."

Though in the back of his mind he'd always seen that as a possibility, the cold reality of the evil they were facing hit him like a blow to the face. "I won't let that happen."

He lifted his head. Ibarra had managed to reverse the damaged car and get it back on the road. He was moving fast enough to create a dust cloud as he drove away.

Kylie followed the line of his gaze. "We can still catch him."

As much as he wanted to stay in the embrace, he pulled free. "We've got to try at least."

They raced to the car. He revved the engine while Kylie buckled in.

The road they were on was more a footpath. He swerved to avoid plant life that seemed to erupt out of nowhere.

Kylie rested her hand on the dashboard. "That car must have been damaged in the crash."

But was the damage enough to slow a determined criminal down? Austin gripped the wheel. "He's headed toward the border."

Austin narrowed the gap between the two cars even though the rough terrain hampered his progress.

The dust cloud cleared as Ibarra seemed to be struggling to get up a hill, backing the car down to get a head start and then revving it. The car made it halfway before sliding down into the drainage ditch. Ibarra jumped out and ran over the hill.

Austin gripped the wheel as his jaw clenched tight. Their SUV had a lot more horsepower than the car Ibarra was driving. He pressed the accelerator, eventually clearing the hill.

Finally the ground leveled off.

He watched as Ibarra scrambled up an even steeper grade toward the Rio Grande River.

For sure the ranger SUV wasn't going to make it up that. Without a word, Kylie opened her door and took off running. Austin was right behind her.

Was she intending to tackle Ibarra? It wouldn't surprise him. He'd never witnessed something as fierce as a mother's love.

He ran until he was close enough to fire a shot. The bullet stirred up the rocky ground around Ibarra, who sprinted even faster with a backward glance over his shoulder.

Kylie ran until she had to claw her way up the steep grade. Austin followed her to the top of the cliff-like rock structure.

The rushing roar of the river surrounded him as he looked down.

Out of breath from running, Kylie rested her hands on her knees—but only for a moment. Then she straightened and scurried down toward the river. He followed, staying close to Kylie with his pistol still drawn.

They searched the high grass close to the American side of the Rio Grande, but somehow he knew they were too late. Ibarra had escaped across the border. Maybe he'd known the location of a hidden raft. Or maybe he'd braved the current and simply swam across. Though Austin scanned the river, no head bobbed to the surface. The river turned sharply. The current could have pulled the fugitive around the bend.

Austin shook his head. Miguel Ibarra had escaped.

Kylie crossed her arms over her chest and stared out at the empty landscape. Her disappointment was evident. "He'll be back across. He's not going to give up." Her voice wavered. "Or he'll hire someone to come after Mercedes and me."

Austin cupped her shoulder. "He was staying in the place next to Limey Pete's. We can get a warrant to search it."

"Well, we can't get that done fast enough." She turned, speaking over her shoulder, her voice filled with determination. "When he comes across that border, I want to be the one to nab him."

"We'll get him, Kylie. One of us will." Though he was

starting to understand her need to protect Mercedes, he was a little concerned that her motherly instinct might overrule her training at the wrong time.

Kylie raced up the hill to the house where Miguel Ibarra had stayed. Austin stood behind her. Brent and Colt were covering the back entrance in case the house had other residents who decided to run or fight back. Ibarra was probably smart enough not to come back there so soon.

She pounded on the door. "US Border Patrol. We have a warrant." It had taken a day and a half to get the warrant. Too long in Kylie's opinion. Mercedes was still safe in protective custody with George and Julie but an urgency to get Ibarra behind bars fed her impatience. She wanted that man locked up, so she and her child had the assurance of safety and could be together.

No answer. She leaned a little closer. Someone was scrambling around inside. "Open the door or we'll break it down." She pulled her pistol from its holster.

Austin pressed against the wall by the door, gripping his handgun.

She offered Austin a raised eyebrow. He wheeled around and slammed against the door with his shoulder. The door was so flimsy it splintered like balsa wood.

"Someone is inside. I heard them," she whispered.

They stepped inside, one after the other, clearing the front room and moving toward the next one. Though they were in the living room, the only furnishings were a couple of mattresses on the floor. Flies buzzed around the dishes in the sink. Empty fast-food container boxes cluttered the floor along with a coffee table propped up with a milk crate.

A ruckus rose up from the back of the house.

Kylie tensed, ready for a fight.

Colt emerged from a back room holding a teenager by the scruff of the neck. “Look who I caught trying to sneak out.”

Brent came down the same hallway. “The first floor is clear. I’ll check upstairs.”

Kylie studied the teenager Colt held on to…just a kid, really. “He might know something.”

Austin leaned close to Kylie. “Why don’t you let Colt do the questioning? You and I can search the rest of the place, see if we can find a clue where else Ibarra might be.”

The suggestion caught Kylie off guard. This was a kid, not a hardened criminal. She was in little danger from him and in most cases, he was more likely to be responsive to a woman asking him questions. Interviewing was what she did best. But while she didn’t understand Austin’s decision, she trusted him enough to follow his lead.

She pulled the picture of Ibarra out of her pocket and handed it to Colt.

Confused, she followed Austin down the hall. The first room they came to had a mattress with a computer on it. Austin slid open the closet while Kylie aimed her gun just in case they had a hider.

The closet was empty.

“I think I would have been of better use questioning the kid.”

Austin lowered his gun and turned to face her. “Kylie, you are the best interviewer between all the rangers and border patrol.”

“So why let Colt take the reins?”

He stepped past her and kneeled down to pick up the

computer. “I just think this case is a little too close to your heart.”

“I wouldn’t have lost it with that kid.” She clenched her jaw. Austin knew what kind of agent she was. Did he really think she’d behave unprofessionally? This was probably about him not liking that Mercedes was a part of her life, thinking that she couldn’t do her job because of it. She felt a surge of disappointment. She’d thought they were making progress in him being supportive when he had expressed some affection for Mercedes.

“I’ve seen agents and rangers backed up to a wall, tired of the lack of justice for way less personal reasons than you have, open fire on a suspect when they could have taken him in.”

She could feel her ire rising, making her muscles tense. “I would never do that, and I sure wouldn’t let my emotions get the best of me with that kid just because he might know where Ibarra is.”

“Kylie, all I’m saying is I saw how angry you were back at the border when Ibarra got away.” Austin held her in his gaze. “I know you love Mercedes. I know you want her to be safe.”

She let out a breath. At least he understood that much. “Guess I was a little out of control.” He was trying to be supportive of her. She saw that now.

“To be honest with you. I felt that anger too,” Austin said. “Mercedes deserves to be safe and to have a shot at a normal life.”

Austin’s voice wavered a little, something she had never witnessed before from Mr. Cool under Fire. Maybe he really did care about Mercedes. Could she open her heart to that possibility? His emotions were buried so deeply, she had a hard time reading him.

"You were not wrong. I was really angry out there at the border," she said. "But I would never let my emotions overrule my training."

Brent appeared at the threshold. "Upstairs is clear. I found these." He held up two disposable phones, the kind drug dealers used. "There's a couple more up there."

Austin stared down at the computer. "I'm going to have a look at this. See if it tells us anything about Garcia or Ibarra."

Brent leaned against the door frame. "If you ask me, we're going about this all wrong. Garcia came across the border to get at his sister. I say if we find the sister, we find Garcia."

"You just have a soft spot for Adriana Garcia because she saved your life," Austin said.

"She did more than that. When the cartel was after me in Mexico, she risked her own life by hiding me in her car and then her home until she could lead me out safely."

"We don't know what Adriana's motives were for coming over here. Maybe she wants to start her own drug business," Austin said.

Brent shook his head. "Maybe she wants to start her life over away from Garcia's influence. I'm telling you she's a good person."

Austin took the computer into the kitchen so he could set it on the counter. Kylie stood behind him as he typed on the keyboard. It didn't look like it was password protected.

In the other room, Colt continued to talk to the teenage boy in hushed tones. The kid shook his head at almost every question. He shoved his hands in his armpits and rocked back and forth, clearly afraid.

Kylie found a cup, washed it and filled it with water

from the sink. She brought it over to the kid. The teen's expression softened when she sat down beside Colt who ran his hands through his dark hair.

"He's admitted to Ibarra staying here off and on from about the time we believe Garcia crossed over," Colt said.

Kylie nodded and offered the frightened kid a gentle smile.

"This is his uncle's place," Colt said.

Austin's voice rose up from across the room. "Kylie, I think you better come here."

The note of tension in his words scared Kylie. She jumped to her feet.

"When was the last time you talked to the people who are protecting Mercedes?"

His question made her throat constrict and her heart pound. She managed a calm response despite the hurricane brewing inside her. "This morning before I came on shift. Less than an hour ago."

Austin pointed to the computer screen. "This is what the owner of this computer was researching."

Kylie stared at the map Austin brought up of Southside El Paso. He zoomed in. Missouri Street. The street where Mercedes was being kept.

He showed her the Google Earth image of the safe house.

Kylie's knees buckled. "We need to get over there right now."

Austin whizzed through noonday traffic. He was having a hard time getting a deep breath. It felt like an elephant was sitting on his chest.

He gripped the wheel and watched the signs on the freeway.

Kylie sat beside him, her hands laced together in her lap. All the color had drained from her face, and her mouth formed a tight hard line. For the third time, she picked up the phone and dialed George's cell number.

Still no answer.

Austin zoomed around several cars, gaining speed as the off-ramp to the subdivision came up. He took the exit, slowing only slightly as he entered the residential neighborhood. The houses out here were far apart and most of them were surrounded by trees and hedges, ideal for a safe house to keep prying neighbors from noticing things. All the same, he didn't want to call attention to the house by having half a dozen rangers barreling through the neighborhood at top speed. Colt and Brent had stayed behind to help Forensics process the house and question the teenager.

After ending the call, Kylie gripped the collar of her shirt and stared straight ahead.

He wanted to tell her that everything would be okay. But he knew that might be a lie. "We're almost there."

She nodded.

He turned up the winding driveway surrounded by trees and stopped in front of the two-story brick house. As usual, the curtains were drawn and the place looked quiet.

"Should…I…go around the back?" Kylie could not hide the fear in her voice. He didn't expect her to.

That was their usual method. Austin was having a hard time thinking straight. His mind was clouded with the memory of Mercedes, the sound of her laughter, how it had felt to hold her that night in the church. The way she had looked up at him, her eyes so filled with trust.

The softness of her fingers touching his skin. All of it made him feel weak in the knees.

"That makes the most sense." He prayed for Mercedes's safety. Maybe they weren't too late. There were a dozen reasons why someone wouldn't answer their phone. "Just in case."

Kylie jumped out and disappeared around the corner of the house. Austin approached the front door with caution. There had been plenty of time for Ibarra to get back across the border or to give the order that someone else storm the house.

Austin peered through a tiny slit between the curtains. He thought he saw movement. A noise to his side caused him to whirl around.

Kylie stood shaking her head. "I can't get in. It's locked up tight."

He approached the front door and turned the handle. Locked, as well. Kylie pressed her back against the wall next to the door, ready to exchange fire if needed. He knocked on the door and stood against the wall on the other side of it.

The seconds seemed to drone on.

He lifted his head. Cameras were installed above them that would have shown who they were to whoever was inside.

The door swung open. Officer George Frank stood with his hand on his gun. Relief flooded through Austin. Now he could get a deep breath.

Kylie stepped across the threshold. "Where's Mercedes?"

"She's upstairs sleeping."

Kylie raced up the stairs.

Austin stepped inside to find Julie, George's wife

and fellow officer, in the kitchen standing by the sink. "What's going on?" She grabbed a towel and dried her hands.

"This location has been compromised," Austin said. "We need to get that baby out of here."

George's forehead wrinkled in confusion. "What? How could that happen?"

The same question had plagued Austin ever since he'd seen the image of this house on that computer. How had Ibarra gotten that information unless there was a snitch inside the rangers or with border patrol?

"Do they have a new safe house set up?" Julie stepped into the living room and stood beside her husband.

"No, we'll deal with that later. I just know we need to get her out of here now." Austin paced the floor.

"I don't know if we can do that. It's totally against protocol," George said.

Their resistance made him suspicious. Maybe *they* were the ones who had divulged the location.

"Kylie is going to be Mercedes's mother once the adoption is complete." Austin shifted his weight. "I think she's the final authority here."

"I'll need to call my supervisor." George moved toward the coffee table. "Where's my phone? I had it this morning."

"Didn't you take that call from Kylie outside?" Julie asked.

At least that explained why they hadn't answered when Kylie called them.

Austin tensed. They were wasting precious minutes. "Let's focus on getting Mercedes to a safe place." He glanced toward the stairs, wondering why Kylie hadn't come downstairs with Mercedes. Kylie understood that it was important they leave quickly.

"And I'm saying we need to clear this first," said George. He moved as though to go to the back door, probably to get his phone.

Austin frowned, not knowing what was wrong but feeling that *something* was off. A thudding noise from upstairs sent his heartbeat to rev up into high gear. He raced toward the stairs.

TWELVE

Kylie had gathered Mercedes in her arms and stepped out into the hallway when she noticed the ladder propped against an open second-story window that led to the expansive landing at the top of the stairs—a ladder that hadn't been there minutes before when she'd checked the back of the house. She saw a man while his back was to her. He must have climbed up the ladder and was searching for Mercedes.

She couldn't get downstairs without being seen. Still holding Mercedes, she slipped into the bathroom and climbed into the tub, crouching and hiding behind the curtain.

She laid the baby down in the tub, thanking God that Mercedes was still asleep. Kylie pulled her weapon from the holster and waited by the door.

The intruder had probably walked past the bathroom by now and was checking the nursery and other bedrooms.

She heard a scuffle and then gunfire. It sounded like it came from downstairs.

Her heart raced. Would anyone be able to come up to help her?

Seconds ticked by. She adjusted her grip on the gun. She eased the door open and stared out into the empty hallway and the open area of the landing. She looked down the sight of her gun and stepped out.

Austin stood on the landing, staring at something behind her as his eyes filled with fear. "Kylie, hit the floor."

She didn't have time to react.

An arm went around her neck as cold steel touched her head.

Kylie squeezed her eyes shut. At least Mercedes was still safely hidden in the tub. Where were Julie and George? Did the noise downstairs mean more thugs had entered the house?

Austin edged closer to the man, demanding that he put down the gun.

The assailant's response was to tighten his grip on Kylie.

"You don't want to do this." Kylie purged her voice of the terror she felt. She repeated the same phrase in Spanish. No response.

Austin took a step toward them. The man pressed the barrel of the gun harder against Kylie's face.

She took in quick, shallow breaths resting her gaze on Austin who continued to hold his gun on the man. He couldn't get a clean shot without risking her life.

Knowing she needed to act, Kylie took a risk and elbowed the man in the stomach. The weight on her temple lifted. Austin moved in and hit the man on the back of the head with his gun. The man collapsed to the floor.

Austin grabbed her hand. "Where is she?"

Kylie pointed toward the bathroom. "Shouldn't we call for backup?"

"I'm not so sure that's a good idea." Austin hurried

toward the bathroom with Kylie right behind him. He gathered the little girl in his arms.

Austin must be thinking the same thing she was. How could Ibarra get the address of the safe house and send this henchman unless he had an inside man or woman?

"I heard gunfire," she said.

"There are others downstairs. George and Julie must be in a standoff with them or they would have come up here to help us by now." He glanced toward the window where the top the ladder was visible. "Get down the ladder. I'll be right behind you," Austin said.

Fear sparked fresh for Kylie. "Holding the baby?"

"We don't have a choice." Austin drew Mercedes to his chest. "George and Julie can't hold off the ones downstairs for long. We need to hurry."

She trusted Austin's strength and balance more than her own. Still, climbing down a ladder one-handed was risky. "You go down first with her."

Shouting rose up from downstairs. Kylie's heart pounded. She pushed aside the encroaching fear.

Kylie took Mercedes so Austin could climb out the window. Once he was on the ladder, he reached up for the bundle that was Mercedes. The baby was wide-awake and looking around. Her arms reached toward Austin.

More noises erupted downstairs. It went against the grain to leave without trying to help the others, but Kylie knew that George and Julie could handle themselves. Her priority needed to be with keeping the baby safe.

Austin was halfway down the ladder when she heard footsteps on the stairs, another man coming up to get at them. The man they had knocked out stirred and groaned. Knowing she couldn't wait any longer, she put her foot through the open window.

She looked down just as Austin's feet hit the ground. "Take her to the car," she told him. "I'll meet you there."

She heard heavy footsteps above her and more shouting. Not George's or Julie's voice. Were they tied up? Shot?

Austin rounded the corner as Kylie got to the bottom of the ladder. A shot was fired at her from above. It hit the nearby ceramic birdbath, shattering it into hundreds of pieces. Dodging the flying debris, Kylie caught up with Austin. She gently took Mercedes and climbed into the back seat. She crouched low just as she watched a man run out of the front door and another come around the side of the house.

She put her body over Mercedes, stroking her pink cheeks and talking soothingly to her.

Austin backed the car out and swung it around with the smoothness of a race car driver. He took the winding driveway at a high rate of speed, barely slowing as he pulled out onto the street. He checked the rearview mirror.

Kylie dared not raise her head. "Are they coming after us?"

"There were no cars in the driveway. They must have parked out here on the street or in the trees behind the house."

"I hope George and Julie are all right," Kylie said.

Austin sped up. She lifted her head to see the skyscrapers of downtown El Paso. Austin worked his way through traffic. She sat up with a glance out the back window.

She gathered Mercedes close to her chest, patting her back and swaying. "What do we do now?"

"We need to get another safe house set up, but limit

who might have knowledge of it this time. Who do you trust on your end?"

She filed through the other border patrol agents she knew. In the years she'd worked border patrol, she'd seen two men turn to aiding cartels and criminals. Both men she had at one time trusted. "I'm not sure."

"I'm in the same boat. I trust my supervisor, Thomas. This time only he will have knowledge of the safe house, nothing in the computer system. That might be the way the snitch is accessing information."

Mercedes wiggled in her arms. "She's probably hungry after her nap. We need to stop and get some supplies."

He glanced over his shoulder and then looked straight ahead. "I think there's a grocery store around here somewhere." He took several more turns and pulled into the lot.

The radio glitched.

"Unit two. This is Colt Blackthorn. Just heard on the police ban there was tussle at the safe house. Are you out of danger?"

"Yes," Austin said. "George and Julie must have phoned it in once all the thugs went after us."

"It sounded like they were a little scuffed up trying to keep them from getting to the baby," Colt said. "But they are okay."

Relief flooded through Kylie. At least that was some good news.

"Look, they want me to bring you in." Colt's voice came across through the static.

Austin looked over at Kylie before drawing the radio to his mouth. "Can you give us some time? I don't want to disclose our location just yet."

There was a pause on the other end of the line before Colt spoke in a halting voice. "Sure. Whatever you need."

Austin might be thinking the same thing she was. The smart thing to do right now was to trust no one. Austin clicked off the radio and stared at Kylie.

Now they suspected everyone. They had to if they were going to keep Mercedes safe. Right now, they could only trust each other. "Let's go get some stuff for this little one," Kylie said.

The grocery store was a mom-and-pop operation with only a few aisles of merchandise. Thanksgiving decorations hung from the ceiling and large signs advertised sweet potatoes and turkeys on sale. Kylie hadn't even had time to think about the holiday. With both her parents gone and her navy SEAL brother out of contact most of the time, friends from church usually invited her over. The holiday would feel empty if she couldn't be with Mercedes. This baby was her family now.

Kylie hurried to the baby section and stared at the items. She couldn't even think what they needed to get. The baby formula she was staring at blurred. She hadn't meant to cry.

Austin stood beside her. "Let me hold her."

After he took Mercedes, Kylie swiped at her eyes.

"Kylie, it's all right. It's a lot to deal with." His voice swelled with compassion.

She tugged on Mercedes's bootee. "I'm just so afraid for her."

He adjusted Mercedes against his side. "Me too." His voice filled with emotion. "We're going to get these guys so Mercedes can have all the opportunities she deserves."

While she appreciated his determination, it did nothing to quell her fear. Mercedes could have died back at the safe house.

Austin shifted Mercedes so he was holding her in one arm. He reached up and brushed Kylie's tears off her cheek.

Mercedes wiggled. "She's hard to hold," Austin commented. "She keeps sliding around."

Kylie let out a laugh. Her spirits lifted. They were cute together, big tough ranger and squirming little baby. "You don't have the hips for it. Let me hold her."

After handing off the baby again, Austin turned to face the wall of baby stuff. "So tell me what we need here."

Kylie focused on the baby food. "She likes bananas."

He ran his finger along the baby food jars until he found the bananas.

Kylie let out a breath and stared at the wall. "And we need bottles and the formula with the blue label. And diapers and wipes. That will get us through the next few hours."

Austin gathered the items and then offered her a soft smile. Mercedes reached out her hand toward him, wrapping her tiny hand around one of his fingers.

Kylie could feel the anxiety and the fear fading away. Something about having Austin close made her have faith that everything was going to be okay.

They got back into the car. Austin drove around until he found a park with a bench that was surrounded by trees to provide them with some seclusion. He held Mercedes while she got water from a drinking fountain and mixed the formula.

Mercedes took the bottle eagerly. The noonday sun

warmed Kylie's skin. She closed her eyes and listened to the contented sucking sounds Mercedes made.

She thanked God for the warm sunny day. If she kept her eyes closed, she could almost believe they were safe—that they were just a little family enjoying an afternoon in the park. That was probably what they looked like to the world.

But when she opened her eyes, the illusion was shattered. Austin paced vigilantly, watching each sector of the park. The strap on his holster was unsnapped, so he could pull his weapon if he had to. Though she thought she'd caught glimpses of the Austin that was so deeply buried, the one who could love and care about Mercedes, he was still all about his job.

Her heart ached as she stared down at Mercedes who closed her eyes while she sucked on her bottle. That's all it was, wishful thinking. They weren't a family, and they weren't safe.

THIRTEEN

Austin felt a sense of relief as they left the city limits headed toward the new safe house. It had taken some convincing, but Thomas had agreed to have this one set up off the books. Though Austin had a gut feeling the rat was either a ranger or with border patrol, Thomas had told George and Julie to tell no one in the police department, either. Austin had suspected them of being affiliated with Garcia's cartel for a moment, but their conduct at the first safe house told him that they weren't involved.

It had taken most of the day to get the safe house arranged. The sun hung low in a sky that glowed orange and pink.

Mercedes sat in the back seat in the car seat they'd gotten for her.

Kylie hadn't said anything since he told her of the new arrangement. When he glanced over at her, she looked tired. All of this was taking a toll on her. He wished there was something he could do for her.

"This is really isolated out here." She angled her head to look out the window at the flat farmland.

The new safe house was out of town surrounded by fields so George and Julie could see anyone as they approached for miles.

"This will be safer for her," Austin said.

She glanced back at Mercedes. "But if there are any problems, it will take longer for help to get here." Her voice sounded strained.

What could he say? He wanted to give Kylie some hope. "The sooner we can wrap this up and get Miguel Ibarra, the sooner you two can be a family again."

She bent her head. "Yes, the two of us." A note of sadness invaded her words.

"Maybe it won't always be just the two of you. When all this is over, maybe you'll meet someone."

She let out a heavy breath and shook her head. "I kind of doubt it. It's a lot to ask any man to take on…my job and a ready-made family." She shifted in her seat and stared at her fingers. "I really appreciate how much you've helped us."

Certainly she didn't see him as daddy material. That was a job he would never be qualified for. But he was glad he was there as a friend for her in this difficult time. "It's what we do, right?" He pulled onto the dirt road driveway that led to the little farmhouse.

George and Julie came outside immediately. Julie's hand was bandaged and George had a scratch across his cheek.

Kylie stared through the windshield, not moving.

"You know, Kylie, even after all this is over, I want to be a part of Mercedes's life."

She perked up. "Really?"

"Yeah, sure. I could be like her uncle or something."

Her expression changed slightly as though a shadow had fallen across her face. "That would be nice." Her voice was flat.

George and Julie waited politely outside the house while Kylie got Mercedes and Austin grabbed her baby bag.

Julie reached for the bag. "You two make a pretty good team. Good work getting Mercedes out safely back there at the other house."

George looked at Austin. "Sorry for any resistance on my part. You called it straight."

Kylie continued to hold Mercedes and bounce her while the baby played with her earrings. She turned her head and kissed Mercedes's cheek. "I'll see you soon, little one."

As he watched Kylie press her forehead to Mercedes's forehead, Austin felt as though his chest were being squeezed tighter and tighter in a vise. Words seemed to get stuck in his throat as he reached over and held a finger out for Mercedes to squeeze. Light sparked in the baby's eyes as she rested her gaze on Austin. An emotion he didn't understand stirred inside him. His throat constricted.

He didn't want to leave Mercedes, either.

Now he understood what Kylie went through every time she was apart from the baby.

After handing the baby over to Julie and kissing her cheek, Kylie locked him in her gaze. "You all right?"

"Yeah, sure. Let's get going." He hurried back to the car as though he could outrun the eruption of conflicting emotions. Okay, fine, the baby had managed to worm her way into his heart, and he was understanding more and more why Kylie felt the way she did. So what? It just made his promise to be like an uncle to her that much more solid. It's not like he was capable of offering anything more.

Austin got behind the wheel. Kylie swung open the passenger side door. Julie encouraged Mercedes to wave goodbye. Kylie let out a laugh and waved back even as her eyes filled with tears. She glanced over at him. "It's okay to be sad about leaving her."

How did something so small cause such a huge tidal wave of feelings? He swallowed hard and gripped the wheel. "I'm fine."

"Okay, if you say so." Her voice had gone all singsongy as amusement danced across her features.

He was grateful for the interruption of the radio. "Yes."

"Austin, it's Colt. You know that storage unit we've had under surveillance for some time? It looks like the cameras picked up some activity a few minutes ago. One of Garcia's known associates just broke into it. We're going over there to check it out."

"We're on our way." Austin signed off and hung up the radio.

"Is this one of the storage units where you think Garcia might be keeping drugs?" Kylie asked. "I remember hearing something about that."

"Yeah, we didn't have enough evidence to search the units, but now we might," Austin said.

The surveillance on several storage units had been set up days ago. The only clue they had was all the units they were watching were rented under the names of dead cartel members or ones who were in prison. Rangers had tracked product—cocaine and heroin—coming across the border that had never gotten out on the market. Garcia had to be keeping it somewhere.

This particular storage unit was in the industrial district. Colt Blackthorn and border patrol agent Greg Gunn waited for them just outside the facility.

Colt approached as they got out of their vehicle. "Surveillance cameras picked up only one man trying to break into the unit."

"That doesn't mean there aren't others," Kylie said. "Garcia's men don't usually go out alone. Cameras have limited range. Maybe it didn't pick up his accomplices."

Kylie was right about that. Garcia's men tended to go out in groups of four or five. "Remember too, this could be a setup to take us out," Austin said.

Greg stepped into the huddle. "This place is surrounded by high fence. The manager gave us the code and hasn't let anyone in or out. We've been watching the gate so we know the man on the tape is still somewhere on the facility."

"Let's move in slow, work our way toward the unit the cameras picked him up on."

Colt pointed. "That's unit twenty-three toward the middle."

"Two by two," Austin said. "Kylie and I will take the west side."

Kylie and the three men entered the gate, securing it behind them and then splitting off.

Kylie took lead, working her way along the metal walls of the storage units. Austin scanned the area around them as well as the roofs of the storage units. Garcia had vowed to take out any law enforcement that got in his way. He wouldn't be above setting up snipers to gun them down.

Kylie slipped around a corner of a building and Austin hurried after her.

"Movement. Back side of unit twenty-five," Kylie whispered. Then aimed her gun.

Twenty-five was an end unit. Sprinting across the path that divided the two long lines of storage buildings, Austin hurried around to the back of the building ready to shoot.

Kylie remained on the other side of the wall.

He scanned the area, which was filled with sagebrush and abandoned scraps from storage units—busted furniture and boxes and garbage bags filled with unknown items. Lots of places to hide.

Staring down the sight lines of his gun, Austin stepped forward. Kylie rounded the corner and did the same thing. At the far end of the line of storage units, a man jumped up from behind a pile of garbage bags.

Austin fired twice, shooting to wound. They needed to question this guy. He couldn't tell if any of his shots connected. The man vanished around the other side of the unit. Gunfire rose up just around the corner.

Heart pounding, legs pumping, Austin hurried after the suspect, knowing that Kylie would be right behind him.

Running in the direction of the gunfire, Kylie hurried to keep up with Austin. He pressed against the wall of the storage unit. She slid in beside him. The area had fallen quiet.

If Greg and Colt had been able to take the man out, they would have given the all clear.

Austin nodded his head, indicating that he was ready to dash around the corner to where the shots had come from. Kylie nodded back. He stepped out, aiming his gun at key spots, high and low. She followed.

He grabbed her, nearly lifting her off her feet, as he slipped between the narrow gap between two unit sections, dragging her with him.

"What?" she whispered. Her heart pounded wildly.

"Shooter on the roof." His whisper was frantic.

They stood facing each other, both of them sucking in air from running so hard. Because he stood a good six inches taller than her, her nose touched his chest. She tilted her head to look into his eyes, remembering how they had almost kissed only days ago.

Greg Gunn ran past where they were hiding. Bullets zinged through the air and sliced through the metal of the storage unit as the shooter took aim at Greg. Austin tugged on her sleeve and pointed. Kylie followed him away from the gunfire.

Austin leaned close to her. "We need to circle around. See if we can catch that shooter on the roof off guard."

They ran back through the rubble on the backside of the property. Kylie heard the sound of footsteps on the metal roof as they rounded the corner once again. She aimed up and shot. The shooter sprinted away from them across the flat rooftops.

Kylie scanned the area around her, aware that the second shooter on the ground might be near. More gunfire came from the other side of the facility.

Austin raced to get another shot at the man running along the rooftops. Kylie spotted movement in her peripheral vision. She whirled around, coming face-to-face with the other shooter as he came around a corner. Shock spread across his face.

"Put the gun down," she commanded in Spanish.

The man held his hands up, still dangling the gun.

"She said put the gun down." Austin had come up on the shooter from behind.

The shooter dropped his gun. Austin moved in to handcuff him.

Greg's out-of-breath voice came across on the radio

Kylie had on her shoulder. "The other guy jumped the fence. Colt gave chase. I'll assist in the vehicle."

Austin leaned close to the man in handcuffs. "Do you know Rio Garcia?"

The man tried to look away. Kylie caught just the slightest twitch in the man's cheek. He *did* know Garcia, she was sure of it.

Austin gave the man a push. "Let's go see what's in locker twenty-three."

Kylie followed beside Austin, aware that the man might still decide to try to flee despite being cuffed.

The lock on storage unit twenty-three was cut through with a blowtorch. No doubt by the thug they had just caught.

"The owner of the storage units said it was a custom lock, which he lets people do," Austin said.

"So maybe there was only one key. The one Carmen said Adriana had in that watch she took when she came across." Kylie pulled open the door and peered inside. Empty.

"Maybe Garcia had a key too," Austin said. "And he took the stuff."

She stepped inside and pulled her flashlight off her belt. "Any news about Carmen's whereabouts?" She turned back to look at Austin.

Worry lines creased his face as he shook his head. "Thomas thinks she is just deep undercover and that we should give it a few more days."

Compassion flooded through her once again for what ranger company "E" must be going through with the possibility of losing one of their own.

She shone her flashlight around and paced the floor.

Austin pushed the man inside and then followed after

him. He spoke in Spanish. "So why did you break into this locker?"

"I don't know nothing," the man responded in broken English.

"We have you on surveillance tape," Austin said.

"The locker was empty when I got here." The man in handcuffs hung his head.

Kylie squatted on the floor and continued to shine her light. She ran her hand over the concrete. "We can get the forensics team on this. If they find drug residue on this floor, that would go a long way to confirming this was the location of Garcia's stash."

Austin leaned close to the suspect and spoke with force. "Did Garcia send you here?"

The man raised his chin and pressed his lips together.

"Not talking, huh?"

Kylie shone the light on their suspect. Was the man acting on orders from Garcia or had he heard about the stash and decided to help himself? Someone had cleaned the place out. Maybe Garcia. Maybe his wayward sister. They still didn't know why Adriana had fled across the border. Was it to get away from her maniacal brother or was it to become his rival in the drug trade?

Austin grasped the suspect's upper arm. "Let's take this guy in. Maybe after we hold him for a while, he won't be quite so clammed up."

They stepped out into the evening dusk. The quiet settled in around them. Their suspect planted his feet and lifted his head, listening.

Rifle shots seemed to come from two directions at once. Kylie hit the ground and crawled toward the cover of the building.

Bright headlights shone in her face. The gate had been

rammed. Two more cars came through it. Shadowed figures got out of the cars and were eaten up by the darkness. At least four men. All her senses went on high alert as she pulled her gun from the holster.

She couldn't see Austin or the handcuffed suspect.

She clicked on her radio. "Requesting backup. We're under fire," she whispered not sure how close the assailants might be.

Maybe Greg and Colt were close by.

Kylie pressed against the metal wall of the storage unit. Footsteps pounded some distance from her.

She took in a breath. It was now or never. Austin might be in danger…or worse.

She worked her way around to the back of the storage unit. Plastic garbage bags ruffled in the wind. She heard footsteps behind her. Whirling around, she aimed her gun but hesitated in firing, not wanting to risk shooting Austin.

Kylie's heart pounded as she pressed close to the storage unit wall and worked her way around to the front side of the unit. Several shots whizzed past her. She heard more footsteps. Men on the run, getting into position. The crunch of metal told her that at least one of them had climbed on the roof.

Her breath caught as she took refuge against the wall. The footsteps were right above her. The overhang of the roof might not hide her. But running would give her away for sure. The man paced above her. Then he stopped.

Her heart pounding, adrenaline raging, she looked up without tilting her head. The slightest movement or noise would expose her position. She could see the vague silhouette of a man.

She lifted her gun and put her finger on the trigger.

An uproar surfaced on the other side of the property. Gunshots volleyed back and forth. A car engine revved. Tires squealed.

The man above hurried away, his footsteps pounded the metal as he ran across the roof. She turned the corner and sprinted toward the firefight. More gunshots, men shouting. The gunfire seemed to be coming from all directions at once.

The headlights of a car nearly blinded her as it sped toward her. She leaped to get out of the way, landing on her stomach.

She pushed herself to her feet.

The car turned around and headed back toward her. She was caught in the headlights as she sprinted toward the shelter of the storage unit wall. A shot whizzed by so close to her cheek that it burned. Kylie dropped around a corner of the building.

Another car revved to life.

She took in a breath and steeled herself. She wasn't about to give up the fight and leave Austin stranded. She darted toward the entrance by the broken gate just as two of the cars zoomed out.

As the dust cleared, she saw that two bodies lay motionless on the ground.

One vehicle remained inside the storage unit.

"Kylie, it's all clear." The voice was Greg's.

Panic surged through her as the dust from the escaping cars settled, and she hurried toward the fallen bodies.

"They shot our tires out. We're not going to be able to go after them." Colt's voice barely penetrated the numbness she felt as she approached the two fallen bodies.

She shone her light on the first body, which lay facedown. A glance showed her that it was the handcuffed suspect. Feeling like her brain was packed in cotton, she moved toward the second body. She shone her light on the man and relief spread through her. Not Austin.

"Three of them got away." Came a voice from behind her.

Austin's voice was like warm honey pouring over her heart.

She turned to face him, unable to hide the affection she felt for him. She touched her palm to his chest. "I'm so glad you're okay. I was worried."

He covered her hand with his, the warmth of his touch soaking through her. She hesitated in pulling away, wanting to draw closer to him and feel his arms around her.

Austin kept his hand on hers and leaned closer. "I was worried about you too."

Even in the dim light, she sensed the magnetic pull between them. When he pressed his lips on hers, her skin felt warm all over.

Over at the car, Greg and Colt lamented their defunct vehicle.

Reminded that they weren't alone, Kylie pulled away. Her head was still swimming from Austin's kiss and the connection she'd felt with him.

She shone her light back on the second man who lay dead on the ground. Even before Austin turned the body over, she recognized the scorpion tattoo on the man's hand.

Austin rolled the man over so he was faceup.

His voice seemed to come from a faraway place. "This is Miguel Ibarra." His words filled with anguish. "I may have killed Mercedes's father."

FOURTEEN

Austin could feel Kylie's hand on his shoulder. "It was a firefight, Austin. He could have accidentally been killed by one of his own men or Colt or Greg."

His gut felt like it was being stirred with a hot poker. Ibarra was clearly not a good man. Why did this death bother him so much?

"What if it was me who shot him?" He knew what it was like to be without a father. How easy it was to lose your way.

Kylie stepped toward him, gripping his forearm.

A moment ago, kissing her had nearly melted him in his shoes. The notion that she might have been hit in the volley of gunfire had made him realize how much he cared about her.

Guilt washed through him. He could never be with her. Every time he looked at Mercedes, he would be reminded of what he might have done. A child as special as Mercedes didn't deserve to grow up with that. Even though Ibarra had been an evil man, no child would want to find out her adopted father had killed her biological father. She might end up hating him if she ever found out.

He pulled away from Kylie, feeling himself growing

cold inside. "All of this would have turned out better if we'd just taken Ibarra into custody."

"He was never going to be a good father to Mercedes," Kylie said.

"There's always a chance of a man turning his life around. I deprived him of that chance." Still agitated, Austin shifted his weight from foot to foot.

"We don't know that you shot him. The shots were coming from all over the place."

"Ballistics will tell us," Austin said.

She took a step closer to him. "Why do you have to know? What is this really about?" Her words held a note of frustration. "Ibarra is dead. Mercedes and I can be together without worrying about him coming after us. We're safe now. That's what matters. Let it go."

Both Greg and Colt must have picked up on the intensity of their conversation. The two men had politely drifted away out of earshot.

Up the road, Austin saw flashing lights that indicated help was on the way.

Kylie continued to stare at Austin, her gaze demanding an explanation. Of course she was confused, his drawing back so soon after they shared a kiss.

Austin took a step back. "I'm sorry. Of course it's a good thing that the two of you are safe now."

Three ranger vehicles and an ambulance pulled through the storage unit gates. Four forensic officers got out of one of the vehicles and proceeded to examine the bodies, take measurements and collect evidence.

Austin walked over to one of the female forensic officers who stood over Ibarra's body. "I'd like to see the ballistics report on this guy as soon as possible, Cyndy."

"You got it," Cyndy said.

When Austin turned around, Kylie had her arms crossed over her chest. "No matter what the ballistics report says, don't punish yourself. It doesn't matter who killed him."

Brent got out of one of the ranger SUVs and waved them over. "I'll give you two a ride back to headquarters."

Kylie walked ahead of Austin. She yanked open the front passenger door. She looked at Brent who had just opened the driver's side door. "Can we go and get Mercedes out of protective custody? I don't want to wait until I'm out of uniform. I want to be with her."

Brent looked from Kylie to Austin. "Tell you what. Why don't you two take the vehicle and go get that little girl. I'll catch a ride in the other car." He tossed the keys over the top of the SUV toward Austin.

Austin caught the keys. He hurried around the front of the car, catching a frosty look from Kylie as he went by her.

Austin got behind the wheel and started up the car. He pulled through the broken gate to the storage facility and out onto the dark street.

"Everybody seems to think there is something going on between us," Kylie said.

"You mean the way Brent looked at us," Austin said.

She nodded. "You must regret the kiss. You're in some sort of emotional lockdown over it."

"That's not it." An image of Miguel Ibarra lying dead on the ground flashed through Austin's mind. "Everything is different with Ibarra dead."

She didn't answer right way. "That's just an excuse." Her words were clipped and severe. She turned her head to stare out the window.

An icy, emotional chill permeated the car.

"The fact that Garcia's men showed up to take us

out means he sent that first guy who we arrested." He knew he was retreating to a safe place, talking about work. "Garcia probably didn't know the storage unit was empty. That means Adriana must have cleared it out before we had it under surveillance."

Kylie crossed her arms and pressed her lips together, staring out the window.

He came to the edge of town. Barren fields clipped by.

He wished she would say something...anything.

The silence in the car was so heavy that he turned on the radio. A sad bluesy tune filled the air, mirroring his emotions.

Maybe Kylie had hoped there could be something between them. He hated the thought of hurting her, but she needed to accept that a relationship between them wasn't possible. As much as he liked Kylie and cared about Mercedes, she had to see that he was not good father material. And now, he had Ibarra's death on his conscience. They deserved better.

The farmhouse came into view. Kylie seemed to perk up as they turned down the dirt driveway. She jumped out of the car almost before he came to a full stop. He watched her run up the stone walkway and knock on the door.

He got out of the car and headed toward the open door.

George was inside fully dressed and holding a steaming mug of something. It must be his shift while his wife slept. Kylie was already out of sight.

George smiled and lifted his mug. "Good news, huh? Kylie went to get Mercedes."

Austin nodded. Ibarra's death still made his gut turn inside out.

"We're going to miss that little squirt," George said.

Kylie stepped into the living room holding a sleepy-eyed Mercedes. “Tell Julie thank you so much for watching my little sweetie.” Kylie kissed the baby’s apple cheek. Mercedes rubbed her eyes. The baby’s gaze rested on Austin and she smiled at him.

Austin felt a tug on his heart as though there were some golden thread between him and Mercedes. He cleared his throat. “Let’s get you two home.”

“Her bag and car seat are by the door,” George said.

Kylie hurried out the door. Early morning light had just started to warm the landscape as Austin fastened the car seat in the back. Kylie gently placed Mercedes in the seat and strapped her in.

Kylie straightened up. Austin looked down at her bright face and green eyes. The kiss that they’d shared back at the storage unit still smoldered in his memory.

He turned away, breaking the magnetic pull of her gaze. “Well, here’s to your freedom.”

“Yes, now the two of us can get back to a normal life,” she said.

As he got behind the wheel and drove toward the sunrise, the phrase “the two of us,” ricocheted through his brain. That was how it had to be. Maybe down the line, Kylie would meet someone. He only knew that he was not qualified to be that someone. Now more than ever.

Kylie’s radio glitched as she patrolled close to the river. Lights across the river alerted her to the possibility of someone making a crossing tonight. Two days after Ibarra’s death, she was working alone. It felt strange not teaming up with Austin, but maybe it was for the best. Just when she felt him opening up, he seemed to shut down. Fixating on who killed Ibarra was just an excuse to retreat emotionally after their kiss. The ballistics report had been inconclusive and Austin still wouldn't let go.

She'd seen how emotional Austin had been when they'd dropped Mercedes off at the second safe house. He cared about her daughter. And he cared about her. Why wouldn't he just admit it?

She clicked on her radio. "Unit seventeen."

The border patrol dispatcher came online. "Agent Perry, are you still near the old salsa factory?"

"Yes, I can see the building from here," Kylie said, turning sideways.

"A car driving by thought he saw lights on inside," said the dispatcher.

"I'll go check it out." Though there had been no activity there in at least a year, the salsa factory had at one time been a drop-off point for drugs. "I'll need some backup."

"Greg is close by. I'll send him." The dispatcher signed off.

Kylie jumped into her vehicle and sped across the desert. As she drew nearer to the factory, she didn't see any lights. She turned onto the road.

The dispatcher came back online. "Officer Gunn is about five minutes away."

"Tell him I'm parked east of the structure." So she'd be working with Greg tonight. That was fine. The less time she spent around Austin the better.

"You got it," said Dispatch.

Before parking, Kylie drove a wide circle around the factory. No vehicles anywhere. If there was someone there, they'd come on foot or been dropped off.

Kylie pulled into the lot and killed her lights. Watching. Waiting. Lights from houses twinkled in the distance, and to the west, El Paso glittered along with the star on the Franklin Mountains.

Already, her heart pounded. This was the first time she'd gone out by herself since Ibarra had gotten killed. Even though she knew he was no threat to her anymore, it was hard to truly feel safe when she was on her own. Austin had been with her through the whole ordeal. She had to be honest with herself. Not being with him left a big hole inside her.

Greg rolled in next to her.

She jumped out.

Greg edged close to her, whispering, "If I remember correctly, there are three floors in there. I'll clear the first floor. You clear the third. We'll meet on the second."

Kylie nodded. She was the senior officer, so she usually called the shots on how a search went down. But the plan wasn't a bad one.

They ran toward the building but slowed down as they approached, watching for activity. Some windows had been boarded up and others had been broken or shot out. The front double doors were at odd angles as though each were hanging by a single bolt.

Greg slipped inside first and Kylie followed. Busted conveyor belts, broken glass and faded safety warning signs filled the first floor. The place hadn't been in use for at least five years, but it still smelled like jalapeños. Heart racing, Kylie hurried up the stairs to the third floor, which had been the administrative offices. She entered a long hallway with her weapon drawn. The first office no longer had a door. She cleared it and moved on to the second one where she stepped over a fallen file cabinet to get inside. One by one, she worked her way through the other offices peering out windows to see if there was any activity down below.

She hurried down the stairs to the second floor, which had been used as a storehouse for ingredients and office supplies. Noise from behind her caused her to whirl around and point her gun. A can rolled across the floor.

Greg came up the stairs. “First floor is clear. Let’s get this done so we can get out of here. This place always gives me the creeps.”

It had never been her favorite place, either. She often wondered if the reddish-brown stains on the wall were salsa or blood.

Kylie worked toward one end of the second floor while Greg moved in the opposite direction. She cleared each of the three rooms and stepped back out into the hallway. She lowered her weapon and stared down the long hallway.

Greg should have been done by now.

Her heart seemed to squeeze tight as she eased down the hallway. The hairs on the back of her neck stood up.

She lifted her gun to clear the first room on Greg’s side of the floor. The next room she came to had a closed door. She kicked the door open. It swung wildly on the few hinges that held it in place.

Her breath caught. She rushed in. Greg lay on the floor with a woman’s scarf around his neck. From the bulging of his eyes, the angle of his body, before she even checked for a pulse, she knew he was dead.

She heard noises in the hallway, someone rushing past. It had to be the killer. Her heart raced as terror permeated her whole body.

She radioed. “Requesting backup at the salsa factory. I’ve got an officer down. The assailant may still be in the building.”

FIFTEEN

Austin pushed the accelerator to the floor and took the corner at a high rate of speed. When the officer-down call had come out over the radio, he and the other rangers had sprung into action. Colt and Brent were behind him in the other ranger vehicle.

His heart skipped a beat. Kylie might be in danger. No matter what, he'd have her back when they were on the job. He zoomed up to the salsa factory, jumped out of his car and raced toward the building. The headlights of the other ranger SUV were still about half a mile away. It would be smart to stay in place until they joined him, but he couldn't wait.

He entered the factory. Metal and wood creaked as wind blew through the dilapidated structure. He wanted to call out Kylie's name. The tightness in his chest would not ease up until he heard her voice.

But knowing that the murderer might still be in the building meant he had to be more cautious.

He worked his way toward what must have been a break or storage room on the first floor. He slipped into the room. Everything was covered in dust except for a torn tablecloth thrown over something. He pulled the tablecloth away to reveal what was probably packaged cocaine.

He heard movement behind him. He whirled around, lifting his gun.

Kylie stood before him. Her face was as white as rice, and there was no light in her eyes. She pointed toward the drugs, a look of confusion on her face. "Greg said this floor was clear."

Austin felt a little hitch in his thoughts. That did seem odd, but he wasn't about to cast aspersions on a dead man without more evidence. "Maybe he missed it." Kylie looked like she was about to fall over. He hurried toward her and gathered her into his arms.

She buried her face against his chest. "I can't believe he's dead."

He rubbed her back and held her close.

He heard footsteps outside the room.

Brent stuck his head in. "We checked the outside of the building for the killer." He shook his head. "Nothing. I better go be with Colt on the second floor and then clear the third floor." He disappeared.

It was hard when any officer lost his or her life. The ranger company "E" would fall apart if Carmen Alvarez didn't get out of Mexico alive. All the other border patrol agents were in for a tough couple of weeks ahead.

Kylie pulled away. "We better get up there. Colt was supposed to be best man at Greg's wedding. This isn't going to be easy for him." She hurried up the stairs.

Despite her own shock and grief, Kylie was thinking of Colt's feelings. He hurried behind her.

"Greg's fiancée, Lena, will just fall apart." Kylie took in a gulp of air and shook her head. "Greg had such a full life ahead of him. I can't believe this is happening."

When they got to the second floor, Colt was standing in the hallway clearly shaken by what he'd seen.

"Colt, I'm so sorry. I know you were close." Kylie stood next to him and gave him a sideways hug.

Colt's jaw had turned to iron. "The wedding was in two weeks." His hands curled into fists as his sorrow transformed to anger. "I think Adriana did this. That's a woman's scarf around his neck. There's a bracelet by the body that looks like the one we've seen her wearing in surveillance photos."

Brent stepped across the threshold. "I don't know if a woman would have the strength to strangle a man of Greg's size like that. I think the stuff was planted by Garcia to frame Adriana. It just seems too convenient."

Colt turned on Brent. "Would you give up defending her all the time? That woman is just as evil as her brother." Colt's face turned red.

"She's not. I'm telling you, I saw something different about her. She saved my life when she had nothing to gain and everything to lose." Brent stuck his chest out and stepped toward Colt, throwing daggers with his gaze.

Fearing that the disagreement was about to come to blows, Austin stepped toward the two men. "Guys, stop. We're all torn up about this."

Both men continued to glare at each other.

Austin got between them. He pushed Brent a step back and then turned to face Colt. "Both of you get some perspective. The enemy is not standing in this hallway. We're on the same team. Texas Ranger company 'E' stays together no matter what."

Colt narrowed his eyes but took a step back. He held up his hands. "Fine." He slammed his fist into his palm. "Let's go out and get whoever did this."

Colt was clearly not in the right state of mind to do police work just now. "Maybe you should take the rest of the shift off," Austin said.

Brent crossed his arms over his chest. “I agree.”

Austin could still feel the tension between the two rangers.

Kylie stepped toward Colt. Her voice was soft, soothing. “Colt, I think it would be best if Lena heard the news from you.”

The suggestion seemed to cause some sort of shift for Colt. The tightness in his expression softened. “You’re probably right about that.” His eyes glazed, the sorrow returning.

Outside, they heard the sound of the sirens coming to pick up the body of one of their own.

The night was far from over. Maybe Garcia had made good on his promise to take out any law enforcement that got in his way and maybe this was Adriana’s work. Austin could only guess.

As he and Kylie made their way out to the parking lot, he knew one thing for sure. If this was Garcia’s doing, it meant that none of them were safe.

Kylie ran through the evening in her mind while watching as they loaded Greg’s body into the ambulance. The killer had to have been lying in wait. And he or she either got picked up by a getaway driver or escaped on foot.

Austin stood beside her. Despite the emotional fissure between them, she was grateful for his presence now. Just standing next to him, their shoulders almost touching, gave her comfort and made her feel safer.

Greg’s death made her think about her own life. She had a baby to think about. Surveillance and monitoring wasn’t as exciting as the rest of her job, but for Mercedes, she would learn to like it so she could come home safely to her daughter at the end of every day.

She waited until they were out of earshot of Colt. "This whole thing felt like a setup. And I wonder why Greg didn't see the drugs on the first floor. Plus, before we even went in, he called the shots for how the search went down. He chose to search the first floor himself." She broached the subject she had been afraid to bring up in front of Colt. "What if Greg did see those drugs on the first floor and he lied about it? It's not like they were hidden real well."

Austin nodded, still looking straight ahead at the unfolding scene in front of them. "It's a terrible thing to accuse a fellow officer of working for the other side—but we already suspected we had a mole on the inside. It's too early to say if Greg was the snitch. We need more evidence."

Kylie's stomach tied into knots. She didn't want to believe that a bright young officer like Greg would do such a thing. "If it was Garcia's henchman that killed him, maybe it was because Greg knew too much."

"Garcia has killed for less. Any man who would put a vendetta out on his sister is pure evil," Austin said. "Those drugs on the first floor will be taken in for evidence, but maybe for now we shouldn't let anyone but our supervisors know Greg lied about them."

The paramedics loaded Greg's covered body into the ambulance and closed the doors. The forensic team had already shown up and cordoned off the factory.

Colt walked toward Austin and Kylie. "I'm headed over to tell Lena."

"I'm sure Thomas would understand if you take the

rest of the night off and tomorrow if you need to," Austin said.

Colt looked over his shoulder as he stepped toward the ranger SUV. "Work is the best thing for me."

Kylie wasn't so sure about that. The death had clearly affected him. She knew from personal experience that it was easy to lose professional perspective when loved ones were put in harm's way. She said a prayer of thanks that she and Mercedes could be together at last now that Miguel Ibarra was dead. But Garcia was still a threat anytime she put on her uniform and tried to do her job.

Austin stepped toward Colt and grabbed his arm above the elbow. "I don't have the authority to make you take the days off, but I think it would be best if you did." Austin tilted his head toward Brent. "I'm sure the rest of the team will agree."

Colt pulled away. "Look who's calling the kettle black. You worked the day after your mother died."

Austin's whole body stiffened. "That was different."

Colt held his hands up. "All I know is I've got to go tell Lena that there is not going to be any wedding or any future with Greg." Colt stomped away.

Kylie edged toward Austin, who was still clearly upset. Greg's death had them all off balance. Not only was it painful to lose a fellow officer, but for Kylie it made her realize just how dangerous her job was. Maybe the same thought was plaguing Austin and Colt.

"This has been a hard night for all of us," she said, hoping her words gave Austin some perspective.

"I don't know why Colt brought that up. It's a whole different thing." Austin's jaw hardened as he clamped his teeth together. "My mother drank herself to death. There was no love lost between us."

Kylie swallowed, trying to absorb the shocking news Austin had shared. "I didn't realize." Austin was such a private man. She knew so little about him. She was even more impressed with the man he'd become considering his background.

"Of course you didn't. You probably had a happy childhood and a great mom and dad." Austin's voice indicated deep turmoil and even embarrassment.

"None of that matters. We're both children of God." She hoped her words reassured him.

Austin let out a breath. "Maybe you thought there could be something between us. I know the thought has crossed my mind."

Hope blossomed inside her. At least he was willing to admit an attraction. It was a relief to know that kiss had meant something to both of them.

"But whatever family plans you have for yourself and Mercedes—there's no room for me in them," Austin continued. "I just don't fit. You and I are two very different people. You're just going to have to accept that all we are to each other are two professionals who work really well together…that's all." He stalked away from her.

Kylie felt like a bomb had just exploded at her feet. What was he so afraid of? She didn't care who he had been or where he had come from. What mattered was the man that he had become. She took a step to run after him, but then stopped. Why bother? He'd made it clear what he wanted from their relationship. No convincing from her would change his mind.

As she watched Austin disappear around the other side of the ambulance, she realized that it wasn't worth the heartache and energy to hope for something more than a working relationship with Austin. Not when he was so completely against the idea.

Kylie stood off by herself as the whirring lights on the ambulance blurred, and she let this new reality sink in.

SIXTEEN

Kylie had just placed Mercedes in her car seat and put the baby backpack in the trunk when her phone rang. Austin's number. She gripped the phone a little tighter. Why was he calling her on her day off? The wound from his clear rejection of her was still raw. Because of him, she had some deep thinking to do about her life and her job.

Steeling herself, she answered, "Hello."

"Kylie, I'm not on duty today. I saw on the roster you weren't working, either."

"I requested some days off." Now that she and Mercedes were in the clear, she wanted time to focus on her daughter. She had also thought not going to work would put some distance between herself and Austin. That had backfired.

"Can we get together to talk about Greg Gunn? I think we need to do this off the record, away from work as much as possible."

Kylie closed her eyes and pushed past her disappointment. Of course this was about work. "Can't we do this some other time? Mercedes and I are going for a hike." It was the first chance she'd had to get out of the house and do something fun with Mercedes. She wasn't about to give that up to talk about work.

"I can meet you there. Which trail are you taking?"

Kyle tilted her head and squeezed her eyes shut. "Aztec Cave Trail."

"I know it. I'll meet you at the trailhead. This is important."

Kylie let out a breath. Austin was right. If Greg hadn't turned on law enforcement, it meant someone else might be the one selling them out. That was information they needed to know as soon as possible. "Okay." She could use the help with Mercedes anyway.

It was a clear, warm day as Kylie drove toward Franklin Mountains State Park. The drive to the Aztec Cave trailhead took all of fifteen minutes from her apartment. The park was one of the few huge acreage wildlands that was surrounded by city in the United States.

She found herself checking her rearview mirror and shaking her head. The car that had pulled in behind her shortly after she left her apartment was still there. It was probably nothing to worry about, and yet it was hard to let go of the vigilance she'd felt ever since she and Austin had gone together to get Mercedes. Kylie let out a breath. All of that felt like it had happened a hundred years ago.

Several other cars were parked at the trailhead, but she didn't see Austin's beat-up truck anywhere, so she parked and settled in to wait, turning in her seat to smile at her daughter who was cooing happily in the back. It felt good to get out of the house with Mercedes. It would take a while to let go of the fear and enjoy her time with the baby. They would have a lifetime of this together. She couldn't wait until Mercedes would be old enough to enjoy things like the zoo and the library.

Austin pulled in beside her and jumped out of his truck. He looked ruggedly handsome in his jeans and button-down denim shirt, which made his eyes look even bluer. He stepped toward her, all smiles. Her heart lurched.

She remembered something her father had said to her when she turned sixteen and started dating. *Some men just aren't relationship material.*

She couldn't let herself forget that, no matter what she felt for Austin and even if she thought she saw fatherly instinct. All he wanted to be to her was a friend and colleague. Now she wasn't even sure if she wanted that. It just hurt so much to be around him. She was thinking seriously about a transfer to another city or quitting.

He looked up at the sky. "Great day for a hike. Glad you're starting Mercedes early in enjoying nature."

Kylie opened the trunk of her car and pulled out the baby backpack carrier. She set it up on the trunk. "The easiest way to do this is to put her in the backpack and then lift the backpack onto my shoulders."

"Got it." He opened the back door and pulled Mercedes out of her car seat.

Mercedes rubbed her face in Austin's chest. He placed a protective hand on her head and looked down at her. "Hey there."

Mercedes tilted her head and stared up at him, clutching the collar of his shirt with her little hand.

Kylie's throat squeezed tight as she pushed past rising sorrow. "I'll hold the backpack while you put her in."

"Maybe I can carry her for a while too," Austin said.

His offer to help made her want to double over from the pain, but she managed a smile. "Sure. That would be nice."

After Kylie slipped into the backpack and tightened the strap around her stomach, they headed up the gravel and loose rock trail. They walked past bear grass and prickly pear cactus. A mist hung low around the mountains like a ballet dancer's tutu. Though the temperature was in the high fifties, the sun shone down on them making it seem warmer. November in El Paso was close to perfect.

They encountered several other hikers heading up and down the trail, some of them with dogs and kids. Kylie couldn't shake the feeling that she was being watched. But when she turned around, all she saw was hikers pointing out parts of the landscape to each other, paying no attention to her at all.

It would be a while before she would be able to shake off the need to be on her guard all the time.

"So what have you been able to find out about Greg?" she asked as the trail evened out, and they were able to talk.

"Not much. I have to be careful how I ask the questions. Colt is still really torn up. How about you?"

"As far as I can tell, Greg never said anything alarming to the other agents. Mostly talked about how expensive and involved his wedding was getting. I know it's not a good time yet to talk to her, but maybe Lena knew something. If he was on the take, she probably didn't know it, but she was engaged to the guy, maybe she noticed behavior that seemed odd."

Austin kept up pace with her. "Maybe after her grief isn't so intense, you might be able to ask her. You're good at getting information from people without setting off alarm bells."

Mercedes touched the back of Kylie's head and made babbling noises. She reached back to pat the baby's hand before continuing her conversation. "Wish there was a way to search his apartment without Colt and the other rangers and agents finding out."

"We'd need some kind of solid evidence to get a warrant. The thing back at the salsa factory is too inconclusive," Austin said.

The trail became steeper as they approached the caves with its two openings. Finally they reached the cave and stepped into the interior. The cave itself wasn't that deep. Several people milled through, looking at the black figures painted on red backgrounds on the cave walls.

Austin turned away from the paintings to face Kylie. "Is it about my turn to carry Mercedes?"

"That sounds like a good idea." Kylie maneuvered out of the baby backpack and helped lift it onto Austin's shoulders. She touched the belly strap. "Don't forget to buckle that." Her hand brushed the denim of his shirt.

He gazed down at her.

What was she hoping to see in those deep blue eyes?

Mercedes patted Austin's dark blond hair. The sight of Austin and her future daughter together caused a new wave of sadness to wash over her.

Mercedes bounced in her backpack.

"Whoa there, little one." Austin laughed as he reached back and patted Mercedes's arm.

The affection between the two of them was obvious. But despite that, Austin had made his intentions clear. She would have to settle for his involvement being that of an uncle.

She didn't want Austin to see her falling apart. "Could you give me a minute? I think I'll go up above to the lookout by myself."

"Sure, no problem. Mercedes and I will explore the cave."

Kylie hurried, climbing the rocks to an area that revealed the sweeping view of the park's rolling desert hills spotted with green and brown and the distinctive Spanish dagger plant jutting above the other plants. Beyond that, the glinting silver of El Paso shone in the noonday sun. A light breeze brushed over her skin.

Maybe twenty or more people were milling around different parts of the lookout. A cluster of ten people stood behind her, enjoying the view. At least another half dozen were positioned at the other lookouts.

She closed her eyes, breathing deeply of the fresh desert air. Kylie heard footsteps behind her as people moved forward for a better look.

She felt a push from behind. She lost her footing. Someone behind her screamed as her face drew closer to the jagged rocks. Kylie reached out to grab hold of something, anything. Her hand grazed rock. She fumbled for a better grip, feeling her fingers slipping.

A face appeared above her, an older man with steel-gray hair. "Take my hand."

He pulled her up as she sought to find a foothold. Below her, rocks crashed against each other.

Once she was on solid footing, she stood up. Her hands trembled. She gasped for air. She could have hit her head on the rocks below and died.

A silver-haired woman stood beside the man.

The older man leaned close to her. "You all right? Those loose rocks can be tricky."

Kylie's heart still raced. "Is that what it was? I thought I felt… Did you see someone come up behind me?"

The man shook his head. "I was looking off that way."

Kylie gazed at the woman. "Were you the one who screamed? Did you see anything?"

The older woman looked at her with compassionate

eyes. "Yes, I did scream, but I only turned around when I heard falling rocks."

Kylie studied the dozen or so people on different parts of the rocks. None of them looked in her direction.

"Kylie, is everything okay?" Austin had come out of the cave and was staring up at her where she stood on the viewing platform. "I heard a scream." Still in the backpack, Mercedes smiled and kicked her legs when she saw Kylie.

Kylie peered down at them as fear sank into her bones. "I think we should go."

Austin studied her for a moment. "Okay, sure. I'll carry Mercedes down to the trailhead."

Kylie climbed down from the rocks and joined Austin. Her feet tread the rocky path while Austin walked in front of her. She was certain she had been pushed. The question was, was it a random act of violence or was she still a target?

By the time she climbed back into her car, Kylie was clearly upset.

Austin stood at her window and touched her arm. "Hey, what happened back there?"

Kylie rested her face in her hands. "I think someone tried to push me off the rocks. I could have hit my head and died."

Tightness coiled around Austin's torso. "Are you sure you didn't slip? Or if you were pushed, do you think it was accidental and the person was too ashamed to fess up?"

She shook her head. "I felt hands on me, and no, I don't think it was an accident."

He hated this helpless feeling. He wanted Kylie to

be safe. Yet, it didn't make any sense. Ibarra was dead. "But why would…?"

"You don't believe me." Her words held a tinge of fire as if there was something even deeper upsetting her.

"I didn't say that. It's just that usually we're in uniform when people decide to take us out."

Kylie gripped and ungripped the steering wheel. "Maybe Ibarra had a cohort who vowed to complete what he couldn't."

Austin could feel himself getting more agitated. What if Kylie wasn't safe? "But it could have been an accident?"

"Would you let go of that idea? I know what I felt." She pulled her arm away from his. "Someone pushed me from behind…on purpose."

He felt such a need to protect her and Mercedes. The only way he could feel at ease was if he could convince himself it was an accident. But he had to trust Kylie's instincts. "Okay, I believe you, but I don't know what we can do about it."

"I'm just so tired of this. I'm seriously thinking of quitting."

He felt a stab of panic. "Don't do that. You're a good agent." He could not conceive of not being able to see her at work.

She shoved the key in the ignition. "There's more at stake than that. I need to go. Mercedes and I had other plans for today."

"Maybe I should hang out with you two," Austin said.

Her expression told him she wasn't crazy about the idea, but knew they'd be safer with him around. "Okay, you can follow us. I'm going to the mall to get Mercedes some clothes. I haven't even had a chance to shop for her since all this started."

"I'll be right behind you." He stepped away from the car and got into his own truck, following her vehicle out of the parking lot.

He scanned the cars around them. She'd been a target in traffic before.

As he thought about what Kylie had said about quitting, his chest felt like it was in a vise being twisted tighter and tighter. Would she still be a part of his life if she was no longer on the job? He'd offered to be an adoptive uncle to Mercedes. Kylie hadn't exactly jumped on that idea.

He kept his eyes on Kylie's bumper up ahead as an emptiness invaded the cab of his truck. If they didn't have work to bring them together, would they talk at church? Would he get brave and sit in one of the closer rows with her?

He shook his head. Why was he even fixating on this? Kylie could quit her job if she wanted to.

Several cars had wedged in between him and Kylie. Then a large delivery truck switched lanes and he lost sight of her altogether. Anxiety made it hard for him to take in a deep breath.

He was grateful when the truck switched lanes again, and he had a clear view of Kylie's car.

Kylie's turn signal indicated she was going to take the exit that led to the mall. He took the same exit ramp.

As traffic slowed, he calmed down a little. Kylie had gone through immense trauma when Ibarra was after her. It was entirely possible she had overreacted to what might have been an accidental push.

He pulled into the mall parking lot some distance behind Kylie. As he turned his car around, he watched

Kylie get Mercedes out of the car and place her in the stroller. He turned the wheel, trying to find a parking space. He drove up and down two rows of cars before finding an open spot.

He saw Kylie pushing the stroller toward the entrance when he got out of his truck. The wind was blowing so hard she wouldn't be able to hear him shout.

A figure in a dark hoodie got out of a car and headed toward the same doors where Kylie and Mercedes had gone.

He eased by the car the hooded figure had been driving wondering why it looked familiar. He heart thudded faster. That same car had been with them on the freeway and parked at the trailhead.

Pulling his phone out, Austin hurried inside to find Kylie and Mercedes.

SEVENTEEN

Kylie watched as Mercedes's eyes grew wide at the bright colors and soft lighting of the mall. Shopping really wasn't Kylie's thing, but she wanted to get Mercedes some new clothes. She looked over her shoulder, wondering what had delayed Austin. The wind had been blowing so hard, it made Mercedes fuss. She had to get inside.

She glanced around at the people milling through the mall. Other moms with kids and teenagers mostly. No one that looked like a threat. But she still didn't feel completely safe, not after what happened at the caves.

She pushed Mercedes toward a department store feeling a little nervous and hoping to spot Austin.

Even though she was grateful for his offer of protection, seeing Austin today had been beyond painful. She'd made a decision on the drive over to the mall. She couldn't be around him. It hurt too much. Though she'd caught glimpses of the kind and loving man he could be, he was unwilling to let her in. The walls always went up with him.

Staying with border patrol in El Paso meant she might run into him. She had decided to put in for a transfer to another border city. It just made sense in so many ways.

She didn't want to stop being a border agent. The attack on the hike was the final straw. If one of Ibarra's cohorts was still trying to get to her, maybe she could escape their reach by moving.

Kylie perused the displays of baby clothes and grabbed a pair of denim overalls and placed them on Mercedes. "You like those?"

Still no sign of Austin. She shouldn't have been in such a hurry to get inside.

Mercedes's bright intense eyes drew her in. Kylie's finger brushed over the baby's soft, smooth cheek. She would raise this baby by herself. That was all there was to it. She'd have the support of the church where she moved. There would be people to help her. But one of those people wouldn't be the Lone Wolf.

Kylie picked out several cute T-shirts with roses on them and a pair of denim pants with reinforced knees. With Mercedes starting to crawl, the extra padding seemed like a good idea.

She paid for her items and stepped out into the main thoroughfare of the mall, hooking the bag of clothes to the handles of the stroller. When she checked her phone to call Austin, it was dead. How were they supposed to find each other now?

On the floor below was a display of tropical fish in huge tanks. One of the rotating attractions the mall had to lure people in to shop. Mercedes was so responsive to color and movement, she might like that. Kylie had been reading in the baby books about how important it was to talk to babies even before the baby could talk, to keep expanding the vocabulary they heard. Seeing the fish would be fun and give Kylie a chance to tell Mercedes about the different sizes and colors.

Her heart felt a little heavy as she pushed Kylie toward the escalator. A picture of her and Austin doing things like this together with Mercedes flashed through her head. She had to let that notion go or she would drown in sadness.

Fear about whether she could be a good mother plagued her, but she remembered her own mom, who had been loving and sacrificial, telling Kylie she had had insecurities when Kylie was little. Every mom struggled with doubt.

The number of people milling around had grown since she first entered the mall. The lunchtime crowd must be showing up to grab a bite to eat or do some quick shopping before heading back to work.

She stood at the top of the escalator, pausing for a moment. When she looked down, she caught a glimpse of Austin staring up at her. She waved. Though she was glad to spot him, there was a part of her that resented needing his protection. She'd had no choice in accepting his protection, but this would be the last time. She needed to cut all ties.

Getting the stroller on the belt was tricky, and she didn't want to scare Mercedes.

What felt like a wrecking ball hit Kylie's back. The escalator belt loomed toward her as she fell face forward. Everything whirled around her. For a moment, she couldn't tell up from down.

The shouts of people seemed to be coming from a long way away. Her vision cleared for a moment. Kylie saw Mercedes's stroller at the top of the escalator and hands reaching for her baby.

Austin had searched frantically for Kylie and Mercedes once he stepped into the mall. He'd just caught sight of Kylie on the floor above him when an uproar came from the top of the escalator. He saw Kylie's auburn hair as she rolled like a rag doll down the escalator.

Austin hurried up the down escalator gathering Kylie in his arms.

She looked disoriented. She managed one word. "Mercedes."

Austin's attention was drawn toward the top of the escalator where a woman was reaching toward a wailing Mercedes.

Letting go of Kylie, Austin raced up the remainder of the escalator, grateful that the other people on the escalator got out of his way.

The woman soothed Mercedes and stroked her arm. "Oh, is this your daughter?"

"Yes." The response was automatic.

"She was just so upset. I wanted to calm her down. I'm a mom myself. I didn't mean to scare you. I wouldn't have taken her out of her stroller."

"Thanks, I've got her." He gathered Mercedes into his arms, drawing her close. Her little body was shaking from crying.

Down below, people gathered around Kylie to make sure she was okay.

He watched as Kylie got to her feet, made her way through the crowd of concerned people and took the escalator up toward where Austin held Mercedes.

"I'll take her," she said.

He passed the baby over, but noticed Kylie was still trembling with fear.

People continued to stare. Some patted Kylie's shoulder and asked her if she was okay.

"Let's get the two of you out of here," Austin said.

"Thank you. I want to go home." Kylie moved away from him. She bounced and swayed with Mercedes until the six-month-old calmed down and Kylie put her back in the stroller.

Maybe she was just embarrassed, but Kylie seemed almost hostile toward him.

He followed behind her. "I saw someone follow you into the mall. Did you see who pushed you?"

"No, I just know I need to get out of here." She rushed toward the exit doors. "When is this going to stop."

"Kylie, wait." He hurried to catch up to her, reaching for her arm.

She pulled away, clearly upset. "Please just help us to get home safe and we'll be out of your hair."

His stomach twisted into tight knots. "What are you talking about? I want to help. I want to be there for you and Mercedes." Why couldn't she see that he cared about both of them?

"Yes, of course…as her surrogate uncle." Her voice filled with anguish. She pushed through the doors and hurried across the parking lot.

Her attitude threw him for a loop, but he tried to be empathetic to the circumstances. "I understand you're upset. What happened back there was very scary."

She stopped at her car and yanked open the back door. "It's not that, Austin." She unbuckled Mercedes from the stroller and strapped her into the car seat before she turned back to face him, eyes filled with fire.

"But you need protection. What happened in the mall was clearly an attempt on your life. We can get to the bottom of this…together."

"No…*we're* not going to work on this together." Her words were as cold as ice.

He took a step back. With her frosty response to him, there was no point in pursuing the matter right now.

Kylie brushed against his shoulder as she slipped past him.

"Promise me you'll get some protection for yourself and Mercedes after I see you home safe." It almost hurt to say the baby's name.

"I will." She got into the car without a backward glance.

He ran up to her window and tapped on it. She rolled it down. "Give me a minute. My truck is parked several rows over."

He stepped out of the way so she could back out of her space, and sprinted over to his truck. As he followed Kylie out on the freeway, staring at her glowing red taillights, Austin felt like he might double over from the pain of Kylie's rejection. He didn't understand. Why wouldn't she want him in her life as a friend? Couldn't she see that was the most he could offer her?

Kylie's face flushed as she stepped into the living room where the post-funeral reception for Greg Gunn was being held. Her eyes met Austin's momentarily as he stood off to one side with the other rangers. Colt had given a beautiful eulogy for his friend. His sagging face and the dark circles under his eyes made it clear that the loss weighed heavily on him.

Austin moved as though to step toward her. She turned away, feeling a stab like a knife to her heart. The last thing she wanted to do was talk to him. All the pain over his refusal to pursue more than friendship was right beneath the surface. With the emotion of Greg's funeral still heavy on her heart, talking to Austin would only stir things up, and she didn't want to lose control.

She was a border patrol agent. Her profession was about controlling emotions. She'd had rocks hurled at her, been called every ugly name in the book by people she was trying to help, but Austin's cluelessness hurt more than all that.

Kylie hugged Greg's mom and stepdad. She'd met them before at a Christmas party. Aware that Austin was watching her, she grabbed a paper plate and mindlessly loaded it up with finger food. She took a cup filled with lemonade.

Lena, Greg's fiancée, stood off to one side. Her eyes were puffy from crying. Kylie offered her a faint smile. Lena narrowed her eyes at her.

All the same, Kylie stepped toward her. She set her drink and food down on a side table.

"I'm so sorry for your loss. He was a good agent and I liked working with him." Now was not the time to bring up her suspicions.

Lena played with the gold bangle around her wrist. Her mouth went tight. "They said you were with him on the night he was strangled."

"Yes, we were clearing an abandoned factory. I wish I could have gotten to him faster."

"I wish you could have too." Lena's voice filled with accusation.

Kylie knew better than to take offense. When an officer died on the job, it was normal for family members to blame the department and the partner. Lena was a woman in pain. If she needed to have Kylie be a target for her grief, that was fine.

Kylie squeezed Lena's upper arm gently. "Let me know if there is anything I can do."

Lena played with her diamond earrings. "People always say that at funerals."

"You're right. I'm sorry. I remember how angry that made me when people said that to me after my mom and dad died."

The apology seemed to soften Lena a little. Her voice lost the sharp edge it had. "Then you understand. What it's like to go through this."

Kylie nodded. She could tell Lena was ready to be done with the conversation, so she stepped away. Looking up, she noticed Austin was coming toward her. She turned her back to him, seeking someone to engage in conversation with, so she wouldn't have to face talking to him. Everyone seemed to be engrossed in visiting. She hurried toward a patio door and stepped outside. The sky was overcast and the wind blew. She drew her cardigan around her.

Because of its higher elevation, El Paso got snow once in a while at this time of the year.

"How are you handling everything?"

Austin's voice pelted her back. She squeezed her eyes shut. "I'm fine."

"I know you don't want to talk to me. I just wanted to let you know we may have gotten a line on Adriana, Garcia's sister."

With the decisions she'd made in the last few days, hunting down Adriana Garcia felt like the furthest thing from her mind.

"I'm glad to hear that," she said, keeping her voice neutral despite the swell of sorrow pressing on her from all sides.

He stood beside her, looking out at the backyard which was simply landscaped with red rock and desert plants. The house they were in belonged to Greg's parents.

"One of the other teams doing surveillance sent us a photograph of a woman who owns a shop that sells Mexican crafts and artifacts here in El Paso. The photo is through a window and at some distance, but it sure looks like Adriana. We'll have to send someone in to investigate."

She couldn't bring herself to look him in the eyes. "Will you excuse me, please?" She moved to slip past him back into the house.

Austin grabbed her arm just above the elbow. "I thought maybe you would like to help out with the investigation."

"I wanted to see the Garcia mission to the end but…" The warmth of his touch permeated two layers of clothing. She locked gazes with him, and decided she needed to tell him. He was going to hear the news sooner or later. "I put in for a transfer to Tucson."

"What?" She read shock and devastation in his expression.

"It solves a lot of problems. I doubt that whoever is trying to take me out in El Paso is likely to follow me to Tucson. They can give me more monitoring assignments and less nighttime work there, which will be better for Mercedes." *And*, she thought, *I can get away from you and the pain being close to you causes.*

Austin studied her for a long moment, blue eyes tearing through her. He let go of her. "I suppose you get to decide what happens to you and Mercedes."

She felt like he was speaking in code. His words were so laden with unnamed emotion. Why couldn't he just say what he was feeling? "Yes, that much is true." She turned to go back inside, half wishing that he would come after her. She found her drink and plate of food on the table where she'd left them.

Kylie took several gulps of lemonade, scanning the living room. Austin hadn't come back in. It was going to take a great deal of time and distance to get over Austin Rivers. She took another sip of lemonade.

She coughed. Her throat went tight. She wheezed in a breath as the room started to spin. Kylie's chest felt like it was on fire. She continued to cough and struggle for air. The plate of food slipped from her hand and scattered on the floor. Her drink spilled as the room spun around her.

Someone had poisoned her. Her field of vision narrowed. Beige carpet loomed toward her.

Austin's strong arms surrounded her. The last words she heard was him repeating her name over and over.

EIGHTEEN

Austin leaned forward and brushed an auburn strand of hair off Kylie's forehead. She looked peaceful as she slept in the hospital bed. But he couldn't shake the memory of the sheer terror in her eyes before she'd passed out. Poison. Someone had slipped poison into her drink at the funeral reception.

Her drink had been sitting out in the open. Anyone could have come by and poured something in. Anyone. Forensics had been brought in to take samples and identify what the poison was. Maybe that would help them figure out who had it in for Kylie and why. Right now, he didn't trust any of the other rangers or agents. Maybe they were on the wrong trail thinking Greg had been the snitch.

He stroked Kylie's hand. She didn't respond. They'd pumped the poison out of her stomach in the ER and assured him that she would have a full recovery. Still, the lump in his throat would only dissolve once she woke up and looked at him with those green eyes.

The news that she had put in for a transfer had hit him like a ton of bricks. Life without Kylie and Mercedes was hard to fathom. Though she said it was for her safety, it felt like she was running away from him. He didn't understand the hole in his heart. What was the hold that she and Mercedes had on him?

Brent stuck his head in. His voice was filled with concern when he asked, “She all right?”

“She hasn’t come to yet,” Austin said. He studied Brent for a moment. He’d always been a stand-up lawman, but that didn’t mean anything right now. Anyone could have put that poison in Kylie’s drink. “What’s up?”

“I need to talk to you.” Brent’s voice took on a note of urgency.

Austin stepped out into the hospital hallway with a backward glance at the sleeping Kylie.

“What is it?” Austin looked past Brent to the waiting room where some of the rangers, agents and people from church were still waiting for Kylie to wake up.

“I meant to tell you at the funeral reception before all this went down.” He angled his head toward Kylie’s room. “A handwritten note was sent to my office.” He pulled it from his pocket and placed it in Austin’s hands.

Austin looked at the outside of the letter. El Paso postmark. He pulled the letter from the envelope and unfolded it. Only one sentence was on the lined notebook paper.

Adriana Garcia is on the Rio Grande.

“Take it in for analysis. Tell Thomas about it. It could be a hoax, but we can’t rule it out,” Austin said.

“And it could be from Adriana. She might be trying to let us know where she is without her brother finding out. Whoever sent this trusts me with the information,” Brent said.

Austin was skeptical. Everyone knew that Brent had a blind spot where Adriana was concerned.

"I think we might be barking up the wrong tree with this Mexican crafts shop. It's not on the Rio Grande," Brent said.

Austin waved the envelope back and forth. "And this could be a total fraud, or a deliberate attempt to mislead us. The photograph is a more solid lead. Thomas made his decision. We're going to pursue that first."

Brent shifted his weight. "Okay then, I think I should be the one to go undercover and see if it's her. Can you put a word in for me with Thomas?"

"She's seen you before. She'll know you're law enforcement and run. You're too close to this, Brent. Thomas made the decision to send Colt in to investigate the shopkeeper."

Brent looked off to one side. "Colt is a mess right now."

"Colt doesn't have the same bias toward Adriana that you do," Austin said. "It was Thomas's decision. Not mine."

Brent's jaw hardened and his hand curled into a fist. "What Thomas says goes, I guess."

Brent was clearly not happy with the decision, but like any ranger, he would abide by the orders of his unit commander.

"Besides, the time away might do Colt some good," Austin added, handing the letter back to Brent.

Brent nodded. "I got stuff to do." He walked away, speaking over his shoulder. "Let us know if Kylie's status changes. We all care about her."

Austin turned back to face the sleeping Kylie. He pulled a chair up and waited for her to wake up. She was vulnerable even in the hospital. No one was going to hurt her. Not on his watch.

He waited through the day. People from church came

and went. A nurse entered the room several times to take Kylie's vitals.

Austin stroked Kylie's hand. "Why doesn't she come around?"

The nurse stepped over to a computer to type in some information. "She's had a terrible shock to her mind and body. Sometimes under stress, people just shut down." She tapped the keyboard on the computer attached to the wall. "I understand she had quite a bit going on even before the poisoning. All that trauma wears the body down."

Austin stared at Kylie's beautiful face. The red hair framed her porcelain skin. The spray of freckles across her nose seemed incongruous to the high cheekbones.

The nurse came over and stood back by the bed. "She'll come around." She rested her gaze on Austin. "You obviously care about her very much."

"Sure. She's a friend…and we work together."

The nurse cocked her head to one side as though she didn't quite believe him. "Is that it?" She turned and left the room.

Austin studied Kylie's soft features. Did it matter if he cared about her? Maybe even…loved her? Kylie and Mercedes deserved better than he could ever give them.

And now it seemed she wanted to push him out of her life altogether. Picturing a life without Kylie or Mercedes twisted his guts into knots.

"Hello?" Mrs. Espina stood in the doorway, holding Mercedes. "I heard that someone was still sleeping. I thought that maybe being close to her daughter might help her wake up."

Austin jumped to his feet and gathered Mercedes into his arms. The baby nestled against his neck. "Thanks for bringing her by and for watching her while Kylie recovers."

"I'll leave you three alone. I'll just be out in the waiting room with the others," said Mrs. Espina.

"Thanks." Austin sat down in the chair. Mercedes studied him while she sucked on her fingers. "Hey there." His heart squeezed tight. An anguish he had never known flooded through him. Could he live without these two women in his life?

Mercedes babbled and reached out for his collar.

Kylie's eyes fluttered open.

Joy burst to life inside Austin. "Hey, you came around."

"I heard my little girl." Kylie looked from side to side, and then sat up. She smiled faintly and reached a hand out toward Mercedes. "What happened?"

"Someone poisoned you at the reception. In your lemonade."

Her forehead furled as a look of weariness fell across her features. "What is this all about? Why is someone out to get me…still? For sure, it can't be one of Garcia's men. None of Garcia's men were at that reception."

"One of the rangers or agents might have been acting on behalf of Garcia," Austin said. "Maybe we had Greg figured all wrong. Or maybe he wasn't acting alone."

Kylie lay back down on the pillow clearly exhausted. "What does it matter?" She massaged her forehead. "It feels like this is not ever going to stop. All the more reason to leave El Paso." She looked at him as though gauging his response.

Her words cut through him. "I'll miss you…both of you."

Mercedes wiggled in Austin's arm and leaned toward Kylie with her arms out.

"Please, let me hold her."

"Are you sure you're strong enough?"

She nodded and scooted herself into a sitting position with some effort. She reached out her arms for Mercedes.

"There's my happy baby." Mercedes tugged on Kylie's long auburn hair while Kylie smiled down at her and smoothed over the baby's silky dark hair.

"You're a natural at being a mom, Kylie."

"Thank you for saying that. I struggle with doubt so much. I want to be the best mom I can be." Kylie gazed up at him. "You're a natural at taking care of her too." She looked away, her voice dropping to a whisper. "We'll miss you when we leave for Tucson."

"Really?" Warmth flooded through Austin and in that moment, he knew he loved both mother and daughter. A seed of hope sprouted inside of him. Maybe Kylie saw something in him he couldn't see.

He leaned toward Kylie. "I really care about both of you." He wanted to tell her not to go to Tucson. To stay here. Could they give dating a shot? "Kylie, I..." She looked at him with her wide green eyes. The words seemed to get stuck in his throat.

She continued to stare up at him while Mercedes wiggled in her arms.

The pastor's wife burst through the open door. "I thought I heard voices. Look who woke up."

Pastor Thorton poked his head in. "We've all been praying for you."

Two other women he recognized from church entered the room and rushed over to Kylie. One of them gathered Mercedes into her arms. "Let me take that little charmer off your hands."

Kylie answered the pastor's questions. Another older

man came into the room. Austin found himself stepping away from the hospital bed as more people crowded in.

Who was he kidding? Kylie didn't need anything from him. She had plenty of people to help her. She'd find a new church family in Tucson and in time, she would meet a man who could truly be the kind of father and husband she and Mercedes deserved.

With a heavy heart, he stepped out of the room and into the hallway unnoticed.

Dispatch came on the line. "Kylie, are you there? Did you hear what I said?"

Kylie's muscles tensed as she inhaled and breathed out a prayer.

Please, God, don't let me die on my last day of work in El Paso.

"I heard you. The monitors picked up movement in sector four." Kylie stared out at the nighttime desert landscape, knowing that violence or gunfire could happen at any moment. She turned and raced back to her SUV. "I'm headed over there. Can I get some backup?"

The dispatcher responded. "We'll send someone out there as fast as we can."

Kylie slipped in behind the wheel and turned her car around. For the last few days sector four had been hot with smuggling activity.

She took in a deep breath to try to release some of the tension embedded in her chest. More every day, she saw the importance of her doing less fieldwork until Mercedes was older.

Since the poisoning, she had remained vigilant and stayed mostly at her apartment when she wasn't working. No more attempts were made on her life.

Now, if she could just get through her last day of work…

Lights flashed in the distance as her SUV bounced over the rough terrain. Someone was definitely out there. Kylie spoke into her radio. "What is the ETA on backup?"

"Working on it."

She slowed down as she drew near to where she'd seen the lights flash, killing her own headlights and then turning the engine off. Kylie pushed open the door and stepped out into potential danger.

She moved slowly, watching and listening—opting not to alert potential smugglers to her location by turning her flashlight on. Her heart drummed in her ears. Where was that backup?

She treaded lightly on the sandy ground, sensing that someone was watching her. She moved her hand toward her gun and slipped into a crouch. Sweat trickled past her temple.

How many of them were out there? She'd seen two sets of lights.

She heard footsteps. Heart racing, she clicked on her flashlight. "Border patrol, hold it right there."

"Holster your weapon," a voice she recognized as Colt's floated out of the darkness. "Everything is okay." His voice sounded light and cheerful.

Confused, she put her gun away.

A half circle of bright lights flooded the whole area. She shaded her eyes with her hand.

In the distance, Kylie heard shouts. "Surprise. Surprise."

Tom Kineer, the senior border patrol agent, came forward and wrapped his arms around her. "You didn't think we were going to let you leave without a party, did you?"

The lights, which were from cars, revealed that a barbecue and table with food had been set up. She saw several of the rangers, including Austin, hanging around the barbecue.

Another female border agent came forward and gave her a hug. "We're going to miss you."

Colt waved at her. "I'm going to get this barbecue fired up so we can get this party started."

"We didn't want the smell of the burgers to give away the surprise." Austin's voiced floated to her from the shadows.

She hadn't seen Austin since the hospital a few days ago. On that day, she'd thought he was going to say he cared about her and didn't want her to go. But once again, she'd read the signals wrong. She had hoped time apart would diminish the connection she felt to him, but it had only increased her longing to talk to him. Several times she'd stared at his number on her phone and thought about calling him. Maybe putting miles between them would make the strange mixture of intense affection and frustration fade.

One of the border patrol administrators hurried over to Kylie. "We've got some soda over in the coolers." She gave Kylie a sideways hug. "You and that little one will have a great life in Tucson."

Kylie snuck a quick glance in Austin's direction. "I hope so." Why couldn't she get him out of her heart?

Kylie mingled and hugged people and took the plate of food Colt handed her. Some folding chairs had been set up while other people perched on the hoods of their cars.

She wandered and nibbled on her food and visited

with people. She found herself being hyperaware of where Austin was at all times. He seemed to be avoiding her too.

Kylie stepped away from the lights of the cars into the shadows. She stared up at the night sky.

Why did her thoughts continually return to Austin? She shook her head and spoke under her breath. "Give it a rest, Kylie."

"Are you talking to yourself because it's the only time you can have an intelligent conversation?"

Austin stood beside her.

"That must be it." Though she tried hard to sound lighthearted, each word felt like it had a weight attached to it.

"So this is it. Your final shift."

She nodded, afraid if she said anything, all the confusing emotions would burst out of her.

"I don't know if you heard but we've been looking at surveillance tapes set up in places frequented by cartel members."

"You spotted Garcia?" It would be nice to know the team was well on their way to taking that evil man in. She was sorry she wouldn't be able to see that mission to completion.

Austin shook his head. "Our computer guy used some facial recognition software. Greg Gunn popped up with suspicious frequency in those locations. It was enough for us to get a warrant to search his place, but we didn't come up with anything more."

"I remember Greg talking about a family cabin. If he had stuff to hide, he might not put it in such an obvious place as his apartment."

"We'll look into it." He stared at her for a long moment.

She really didn't want the conversation to become per-
onal. "I hope the team is able to get to the bottom of it."

"I wish you were giving us a hand," Austin said.

The affection in his voice made her take two steps
ack. Images of all they had been through together and
he kiss they'd shared welled up. In her mind's eye, she
aw Austin holding Mercedes, smiling at her. The pain
ame out as anger. "Well, I'm not. I'm leaving." *Because
very time I see you, you break my heart.*

Colt stepped toward them. "Hey, don't go hogging
Kylie all to yourself. We're all going to miss her. Why
don't you two come back to the party?"

"Good idea." Kylie stepped back toward the lights and
he crowd without a backward glance to Austin.

NINETEEN

It was dusk by the time the warrant to search Greg's family cabin came through. Austin and Brent arrived just as the sky had turned a charcoal gray. A chill wind hit him as Austin opened the door. Because they were in high desert, temperatures could drop dramatically at night.

The men made their way up the stairs and stepped across the porch. Noises from within the cabin caused Austin to rest his back against the wall by the door. Brent did the same on the other side of the door. Austin rolled along the wall until he had a view of the interior of the cabin through a window with a curtain partially pulled back. Movement flashed past his field of vision.

Austin pulled his weapon before twisting the doorknob and pushing the door open, ready to fire. The noise of things being tossed around, rose up from a far room. Austin and Brent made their way toward the room with a closed door.

"Texas Rangers. Come out with your hands up."

The noise stopped.

A moment later, a car parked in back fired up.

The men barged into the room, which was a combination office and storage room for outdoor gear. A file cabinet was flung open and the computer was on.

Austin ran to the window. He recognized the car. It belonged to Lena, Greg's fiancée.

"Hey, Austin." Austin turned back to face Brent who held out a photograph to him. "She must have dropped it."

The photo was grainy but it was clearly of Kylie and Valentina, heads close together, conversing on a city street. So Greg *had* been the double agent. He must have had Kylie under surveillance when he was off duty and taken the photo to tag Valentina as her informant.

Brent continued to search the room. "She came here to destroy evidence. For what? Out of loyalty?"

Austin's thoughts raced. The strongest motivator for an agent to sell information was greed. But it was Lena who had the expensive taste, not Greg. Maybe she was involved.

He stared down at the photograph of Kylie and Valentina. He'd overheard them talking at the reception and knew that Lena blamed Kylie for Greg's death. The attempts on Kylie's life, pushing and poisoning, were something typically a woman would do. "I'm going after her. I might be able to catch her." Just how vengeful was Lena? Angry enough to take out Kylie and not care if Mercedes was collateral damage?

"I'll stay here and get the forensics team to come in. Maybe she left other evidence behind," Brent said. He held up his phone. "We can get highway patrol to be on the lookout for her vehicle."

Austin hurried out to the SUV and jumped in. Lena had about a five-minute start on him, but there was only one road leading up to the cabin. He gunned his engine and took the curves on the dirt road at a dangerous speed.

He caught a glimpse of Lena's dust cloud when

the road straightened out but couldn't spot the car. He gripped the wheel as the needle edged past fifty miles an hour on the curving section of road.

He felt a sense of urgency and concern for Kylie's and Mercedes's safety. Lena knew they were on to her. She wouldn't care about taking things slowly or covering her tracks anymore.

Down below, he saw where the dirt road joined with the highway. Lena's blue Lexus was swallowed up by a cluster of cars. Tracking her now would be hard. All the same, he pressed the accelerator and headed down toward the highway. Choosing a gap in the cars and merging with the traffic, he headed back toward El Paso.

Austin wove in and out of traffic. He spotted the Lexus only once and then lost it when she slipped out of view after passing a semi truck. Brent had probably already phoned headquarters so they would have alerted highway patrol to be on the lookout for her car. Chasing after her himself would be a waste of time. If he really wanted to help, he needed to warn Kylie.

Austin knew the last person Kylie wanted to hear from was him. But she needed to know that she was in danger. The outskirts of El Paso came into view.

He tried Kylie's number. The phone rang five times before going to message. "Kylie, this is Austin. Listen, I think Lena might have had something to do with the attempts on your life. If she comes anywhere near you, don't trust her. Give me a call. I just need to hear your voice."

It was possible she was so busy packing, she hadn't heard the phone or had chosen to ignore it when she saw it was Austin's number. Austin decided he needed to swing by and make sure Kylie was okay.

He took the exit off the freeway that was close to Kylie's place. He would endure Kylie's anger if it turned out Lena had simply flown the coop instead of seeking revenge. He just needed to know she and Mercedes were safe.

Up ahead, a street was closed off to dig up a sewer pipe. Austin rerouted himself and zigzagged through a residential area to get back on the main thoroughfare that led to Kylie's apartment complex. The detour had cost him about ten minutes.

His phone rang. Kylie. He let out a breath as the tightness in his chest subsided.

Kylie's voice sounded a little cold. "I saw you called. I was busy packing."

"Did you hear the message?"

"No. I've been busy. Just a second. That's the door."

Austin listened as he heard voices, a conversation that was too far from the phone for him to follow.

Then Kylie shouted. "Lena, you don't want to do this!"

Austin's heart skipped a beat. Kylie was in trouble and she was letting him know it.

Austin pressed the gas as he raced through the city, praying that Kylie and Mercedes were still alive.

Lena held a gun on her. Kylie's first thought was that Mercedes was in the next room playing in her crib. She needed to protect her baby at all costs.

Kylie put her phone on an entryway table and held her palms toward Lena. "Lena, you don't want to do this." The phone was still on. Maybe Austin would hear what was going on.

"Sure I do. You destroyed the great life Greg and I were setting up. Why didn't you have Greg's back?"

This was her chance to find out why Greg had really

been killed. "I followed standard protocol. Greg died because of who he was really working for."

"We had to do it. His pay was an insult. The cartel gave us the money we deserved."

"Was that you who pushed me and poisoned me?" Kylie's heart beat out a wild rhythm.

"Pathetic attempts. Took me a while to find Greg's gun at the cabin."

Kylie focused on Lena's face while looking for an opening that would be enough for Kylie to use her training to disable Lena. She chose her words carefully, hoping to provoke Lena into making a mistake. "Maybe if Greg hadn't felt so much pressure from you to live the high life, he would still be alive today."

Lena's face turned beet red as she raised the gun.

Kylie dove toward Lena's hand to try to force Lena to drop the weapon. The two women struggled. It went off.

Kylie squeezed Lena's wrist on the nerve endings until she dropped the gun. Both women scrambled for the gun, which slid across the wood floor underneath the couch. Lena snatched a lamp off a side table and crashed it against the side of Kylie's head. Lena crawled across the floor and retrieved the gun.

Mercedes cried from the next room.

No, dear God, no.

"Ha." Lena burst to her feet and stomped into Mercedes's bedroom.

Despite the overwhelming panic and dizziness from being hit, Kylie pushed herself to her feet and hurried after Lena. Lena was leaning over the crying baby when Kylie stepped into the room. "Don't you touch her."

"I'll do what I want." Lena's eyes flared with anger and she pointed the gun at Kylie.

Mercedes reached for Kylie. She didn't dare move toward the crib while the gun was aimed at her, so she tried to comfort her daughter with her voice. "It's all right, baby girl. I'm right here."

Mercedes cried even louder, arching her whole body backward.

"Don't hurt her." Mercedes's crying made Kylie's heart squeeze tight.

Lena scowled at her. "Come over here and get this kid before she gives me a headache."

Kylie rushed over and lifted Mercedes out of the crib, holding her close and making soothing sounds even though her own heart was pounding with fear.

When she looked up, Lena held the gun on both of them. "You're going to get in your car and you're going to drive. Do you hear me?"

Kylie nodded, wondering exactly what Lena had in mind.

Lena held the gun close to her body so no one would notice it as she forced Kylie to walk out to her car. Kylie glanced side to side, but there was no one she could call to for help. No one was around at this hour. It was getting dark and people were probably inside eating dinner.

She placed Mercedes in her car seat. The baby kicked her legs, trying to get Kylie to smile. Kylie's eyes warmed with tears as she leaned in and kissed her baby on the forehead. She ran a finger down Mercedes's cheek, saying a prayer that they would both get out of this alive.

Lena's words pelted her back. "Get in the car and drive."

As she climbed in behind the wheel, Kylie fumbled with the keys, trying to control the tremble in her fingers.

Lena slid into the passenger side of the car and pointed

the gun at Kylie. "Now drive out of the city into the desert. I'm sure you know lots of good places where no one can find two bodies."

So that was it. Lena was going to kill both of them.

"Lena, why are you doing this? Do you really want to face a murder rap? You could walk away right now with no charges against you."

"I'm a bookkeeper, who do you think kept track of the money?" Lena bent toward Kylie and poked the barrel of the gun into her upper arm. "Thanks to you and your friends poking around, all of it is going to come out." Lena spat out her words.

"Please, kill me if you must. You'll have to drive the car back out of the desert. Just abandon the car and leave Mercedes in it. Someone will find her." She prayed it would be someone who wouldn't harm her baby. "Or let me leave Mercedes in the apartment, please." It was the only chance she had to save Mercedes. "She's innocent."

Lena unbuckled her seat belt and pressed even closer to Kylie so her mouth was inches from Kylie's ear. "You took away someone I loved. So I'm going to take away someone you love. Then you'll know how it feels. Now drive."

After a few minutes, Lena stared out the window and then poked Kylie with the gun. "I have a better idea. Take me to where Greg died."

Tears streamed down Kylie's cheeks as she fought off the despair that consumed her. She stared through the windshield as the city clipped by. There was still a chance for her and her baby to get out alive. They were both still breathing. God was in control. Evil could not prevail. She would come up with a plan.

The buildings grew farther apart when they came to the edge of the city and desert stretched before her.

Mercedes made ooh and ahh sounds from the back seat. Kylie squeezed her eyes open and closed real fast, pushing past the sense of doom that seemed to surround her. Mercedes's innocent voice was like knife slices on her skin, knowing it was her fault that her precious little girl was in danger.

Though she could feel hope fading, she wasn't about to give up. Kylie checked the rearview mirror. No one was behind them.

It was up to her to save herself and Mercedes before this woman, blinded by rage and grief, put bullets in both of them.

TWENTY

When Austin pulled up to Kylie's apartment complex, her car was five blocks ahead of him and about to turn a corner. Lena's Lexus was parked on the street. Kylie was clearly in danger. His guess was the two women and the baby were in that car. He could only imagine what Lena had in mind. He hung back, not wanting to alert Lena that she was being followed. He thought about calling for backup, but worried that it might spook Lena into lashing out. Better to figure out where she was going, and then form a plan to neutralize the danger.

When the car turned the corner, he sped up. He followed them through residential streets until it was clear they were headed for the edge of the city. He knew the streets well enough to intersect them. They sped past him while he waited at a stop sign. He caught a quick glimpse of Kylie at the wheel. There were enough cars on the road that he could stay back and still track them. As they got farther out of town and traffic thinned, he slowed down but still kept the car in sight.

Now he knew where they were going, toward the old salsa factory where Greg had been shot.

Austin clicked on his radio. "Requesting backup.

Kylie and daughter believed to have been abducted by Lena Norton, who is likely armed and dangerous. Headed up Old Millhouse Road toward the salsa factory." He gave the dispatcher the license number and description of Kylie's car.

He turned abruptly onto a dirt road that was overgrown. He knew a cross-country shortcut to the factory that Kylie had talked about on one of their surveillances together.

The SUV bounced along the rutted road. He let up on the gas. The road was rougher than he'd expected, forcing him to go slower. It was too late to turn back. He prayed his decision wouldn't cost Kylie and Mercedes their lives.

"I think this is a fitting place for you to die, don't you?"

Kylie pulled up to the salsa factory. Tears flowed down her cheeks as she struggled to get a deep breath. She caught a glimpse of Mercedes in the back seat. "Please, you haven't thought this through. They'll catch you."

"That is where you are wrong. I learned all about how you guys work from Greg. They will find your car miles from here, which will lead them off the trail. Thanks to Garcia, I have friends in low places who will pick me up. After that, I have enough money so I can just disappear."

"Please." Kylie felt like her spine was being shaken from the inside. "At least let Mercedes live. Take her to a fire station. For the love of God, she's just a baby."

Lena seemed unmoved by Kylie's plea. "I would have gotten out of El Paso much sooner, if it wasn't for the unfinished business of making you suffer like I've suffered. Plus, leaving too soon would have cast suspicion on me." Lena waved the gun. "Keep your hands on the wheel. Don't get out of the car until I do."

Lena trained the gun on Kylie while she pushed the door open and hurried around to the driver's side. "Now open your door and toss me the keys." Kylie pulled the keys out of the ignition.

There would be no chance of escape once she gave up the keys.

"Hurry up." Lena moved in and pointed the gun through the window at Mercedes.

The woman's eyes were wild. Lena was beyond being able to reason with.

Kylie tossed the keys out on the ground. Still pointing the gun at Kylie, Lena backed up, picked up the keys and put them in her jacket pocket.

Kylie's heartbeat drummed in her ears like a funeral dirge. Once she was holding Mercedes, there would be no opportunity to take Lena out. But there was nothing stopping Lena from firing at any moment if Kylie didn't cooperate. So she followed the instructions to get out of the car. Go to the back seat. Open the door to take out Mercedes.

Mercedes smiled at her. Kylie's gaze darted around the back seat, searching for a weapon, until she saw a window scraper used for the rare times it snowed in El Paso.

"Come on. Hurry up," Lena said.

Kylie mimed unbuckling Mercedes while she picked up the scraper, whirled around and threw it at Lena like a boomerang. The scraper hit Lena in the forehead, stunning her for a moment. Kylie dove toward her, knocking her to the ground. The two women wrestled. Lena slapped Kylie's face and pulled her hair. Her eyes watering, Kylie flipped over on her stomach and tried to crawl away.

Lena grabbed her foot.

Rage like she had never known surged through Kylie. No one was going to hurt her daughter. She kicked Lena hard in the nose.

Lena screamed in pain, placing her hand on her nose and turning away.

Kylie searched frantically for the gun, which Lena must have dropped. She didn't see it anywhere, but the glint of metal from the setting sun caught her eye. The keys. They must have fallen out of Lena's pocket. Kylie picked them up and raced back toward the car.

She jumped in and twisted the key in the ignition. The car roared to life as she slammed the door. Lena had recovered and was standing holding the gun.

Kylie hit the gas. Shots shattered the back window.

Mercedes cried out. Kylie glanced over her shoulder. The baby was alive.

More shots echoed through the car. The car jerked and slowed as the back tires deflated.

"Come on." Kylie pressed the gas out of sheer desperation, even knowing that she couldn't reach the road. She wouldn't be escaping in the car with two flat tires.

She was so grateful for the sound of Mercedes crying. It meant the bullets hadn't found her baby. When she glanced back, she saw no crimson stain on Mercedes. The cry sounded more like it stemmed from fear rather than pain.

Please, God, don't let her be hit.

The car jerked forward then stopped altogether. Lena was running toward her.

Kylie jumped out of the car, hoping to keep Lena from getting to Mercedes.

Lena fired another shot while she ran toward Kylie. The shot went wild.

How many rounds had been fired? Four, maybe five. Kylie ran toward the factory. It was a risk. What if Lena decided to hold Mercedes hostage instead of chasing after her? Lena touched off two more rounds. Kylie dove to the ground, hoping Lena would fire again and use up her bullets.

Lena stalked toward Kylie. A handgun was only good at close range. All Kylie had to do was keep some distance between herself and Lena.

Kylie jumped up and ran toward the next bit of cover, a pile of twisted metal. Lena took the bait and fired off two more shots. Kylie ran into the building and pressed against a wall. Lena had one, maybe two shots left.

Kylie heard footsteps coming toward her. Then they stopped.

Kylie took in a breath that felt like it had sharp edges on it.

She didn't hear retreating footsteps. That was a good sign. Lena was in the building too.

Then Kylie saw the glow of headlights in the distance coming from the back side of the factory where the wall had been torn away. Maybe Austin understood her message on the phone and called the police. But how would they know to find her at the salsa factory?

"It's over, Lena. Help is on the way," she bluffed.

"How do you know that's not one of my friends?" From the breathlessness of her words, Lena was in motion again. "You know what this old building is used for. All the cartels know about it."

Kylie fought off the encroaching fear. If those headlights were Lena's cohorts, she didn't stand a chance. She angled her body to get a location on Lena.

The woman was sprinting back toward Kylie's car. Kylie took off at a dead run, grateful for the physical conditioning her job required that allowed her to close the distance between herself and Lena. Mercedes's crying seemed to surround her like some sort of drumbeat. Kylie leaped through the air and tackled Lena. Lena flipped around on her back and struck out at Kylie. Too late, Kylie realized that the gun was in her hand—positioned as a bludgeon that Lena slammed into Kylie's temple.

Kylie's field of vision started to close in on her. She willed herself not to pass out. Even as her vision went black, she could hear Mercedes's plaintive and frightened cry.

Austin hurried around the factory with his gun drawn. Lena had just pulled herself to her feet and was looming over the fallen Kylie who lay facedown.

"Back off, Lena." Austin spoke with authority, though he was scared to death he was too late. "Drop the gun."

Lena snarled at him, but complied and held her hands up in the air.

The sound of Mercedes crying was like music to his ears. The baby was okay.

Austin moved in and handcuffed Lena. Kylie still wasn't moving. Up the road, he spotted the glow of headlights. His backup was on the way.

"Get down on your knees and don't move," he ordered, still training the gun on Lena. "Right there, where I can see you."

Still keeping an eye on Lena, Austin leaned down and touched Kylie's bloody cheek. The tension in his chest let up a little. She was still breathing. "Kylie?"

Two other ranger vehicles pulled into the overgrown parking lot. Men jumped out and ran toward Lena.

Austin held Kylie in his arms. He brushed his hand over her uninjured cheek. "Kylie, please wake up."

Her eyes fluttered open. "Mercedes?"

"She's okay." His throat grew tight from the rush of joy flooding through him. "You're both going to make it."

"Thanks for coming for me." Affection gave her words a smoldering warm quality.

"It's what we do, right?" The moment he said the words he regretted them. He didn't come to her rescue because she was a colleague, which meant they were supposed to have each others' backs. He came for her because he loved her and Mercedes.

Her expression clouded and her words became frosty. "Yeah, sure…right." She pulled herself to her feet. "Just for old times' sake before I leave."

He caught the flash of pain in Kylie's face.

Kylie stumbled a little as she made her way back to her car, which had two flat tires. She reached into the back seat.

"Good work." Colt stood beside Austin, arms crossed over his chest. "Looks like we got her. Kylie's safe now."

"Yeah, I guess we got here just in time." Austin watched as Kylie pulled Mercedes out of her car seat and enveloped her in her arms. She turned away from Austin.

The tightness invaded his chest all over again, but this time for a different reason. Why couldn't he just tell her how he felt?

Colt nodded as he watched Lena being led away. “Yeah, I’d say we got here just in time.”

Somehow though, Austin had a feeling where he and Kylie were concerned, he was too late.

TWENTY-ONE

Kylie looked at the calendar on her phone and the piles of boxes that surrounded her in her apartment. Today was Thanksgiving Day. She'd made no plans at all. She'd thought she would be in Tucson by now, starting a new life with Mercedes.

Somehow, while dealing with filing reports about Lena and all the excitement involved with uncovering everything Lena and Greg had done, she'd neglected to schedule the movers. Now they would not be able to come until Monday.

Mercedes bounced in her walker and tilted her head to one side.

"Our first holiday together as a family." From the floor where she was crouching, she reached out for Mercedes's soft hand. "Not that you're going to remember it. I just wanted to make it special."

People at church probably thought she was gone by now. She'd already said her goodbyes. She rose to her feet and stared into her nearly empty refrigerator. Nothing but convenience stores would be open.

She swiped through her phone until her camera came up. "Who cares where we are or what we're doing as long as we are together." She focused in on Mercedes. "Smile."

"Years from now, when you look at this picture, I will tell you that it was our first Thanksgiving together." She poked Mercedes in the belly and made a funny noise so the baby laughed. "You had baby food bananas and I had tuna out of a can."

Mercedes's smile lit up the whole room and sent sparks through Kylie's heart. And in just a few more days, they would start their new life. She let out a heavy breath. Why, then, did she feel such a heaviness, like there was incomplete business between her and Austin?

She was leaving loose ends in more ways than that. Garcia was still at large and so was his sister, Adriana, though Colt was chasing down the lead of the woman who owned the Mexican crafts store and who was believed to be Adriana.

Also, it weighed heavily on her that the ranger Carmen Alvarez had still not made contact. Was one of the few female rangers dead or just deep undercover? As far as they could tell, Greg hadn't sold Carmen out to the cartel, but they hadn't gone through all of the evidence yet.

So much unfinished business that she wouldn't be able to see to the end.

Though it bothered her, she knew where her priority needed to be. She lifted Mercedes up, twirling and dancing with her as she hummed a slow sad tune. She wanted her baby to have all the best things in the world—including the best father. And she'd really thought Austin might fit in that role. Too bad he seemed to think otherwise.

She'd spent all this time reading into Austin's expressions and reactions. Though he had admitted an attraction to her, and had clearly bonded with Mercedes, he had been unwilling to move forward. In all that he'd done for them, he had shown that he at least felt the need to protect them. Didn't that show that he cared? Some men were men of action, not of words.

She stopped and stared out a window that overlooked the park that bordered the apartment complex. A man and a woman walked by. The woman pushed a stroller while the man held a toddler in his arms. A sweet scene unfolding that just made her sad.

Austin was a man whose heart was buried too deeply for her to access. Why couldn't he just admit how he felt?

Mercedes grabbed Kylie's cross necklace and tugged. "Hey you. That's Mommy's." Kylie spoke in a gentle tone. Though the adoption would not be complete for several more months, she truly felt like Mercedes's mother.

Mercedes nestled into Kylie's neck. Kylie breathed that sweet baby smell as Mercedes's soft hair brushed her cheek.

The doorbell rang.

Only a handful of people knew that she hadn't left for Tucson yet. She hurried across the room and swung the door open.

Austin stood there with a box filled with food. An older, shorter man leaned in close beside him.

"Heard you got delayed by red tape. Thought you could use a little Thanksgiving cheer. Bachelor style."

Kylie looked down into the box, which contained mostly canned goods.

The older man stepped forward. "One of the ladies at the retirement villa baked me up an apple pie."

"I like apple pie way better than pumpkin." Kylie couldn't hide her gushing. Her spirits were lifted by such a kind gesture.

The older man stepped past Austin and held out his

hand. "I'm Robert Wilson. Years ago, I was Austin's probation officer."

"Now he's my family." Austin's blue eyes seemed full of light and life.

Kylie stepped to one side so the men could come in. Austin put the box on the counter. Despite their tattered relationship, Kylie was grateful to have company for Thanksgiving. It made leaving seem less sad and gave her hope that maybe she and Austin could find some closure.

"We'll have to eat on the floor. I sold my couch and dining room table yesterday," Kylie said.

Robert rubbed his hands together and winked at Kylie. "I always did like picnics."

"My dishes are packed."

Austin dug into the box and held up some paper plates.

Mercedes reached out for Austin.

Kylie thought she would fall over from the pain the gesture caused. Mercedes loved Austin.

"I can take her," Austin said.

Was that a waver she'd heard in his voice? Or was it just her wishful hoping? She passed over the baby. "I'll get things ready." Kylie locked on to Austin's gaze and then looked away.

She busied herself in the kitchen. Opening cans of cranberries and a package of sliced deli turkey.

Robert laid out one of Mercedes's blankets in the middle of the living room surrounded by boxes while Austin walked around bouncing Mercedes and talking to her. Mercedes cooed and babbled. After seeing that there was a can of green beans, she searched through the boxes for a pan to heat them up in. On her way back to the kitchen, she watched Austin press his forehead against Mercedes's and then pull the baby close, rubbing her back.

Kylie pushed aside the desire to read into what the gesture had meant.

Austin looked over at Kylie. "I'm going to miss her. I'm going to miss both of you."

Kylie felt a tug on her heart as though an invisible golden thread joined her and Austin. She knew in her heart if he'd just tell her he loved her, she'd stay. But that wasn't going to happen.

She needed to get beyond all this speculating and all this hoping…it only led to heartache.

"I guess it's just how it has to be." She returned to the kitchen to put food on plates. Her throat was tight as she swallowed to get rid of the lump forming there. It was going to take a lot of time and a lot of miles between them before she was over Austin and what might have been.

Kylie looked so beautiful with her auburn hair framing her pale face. Austin watched her as she worked. When he tried to picture his life without her and Mercedes, all he saw was blackness.

"Can I give you a hand with anything?" Robert had gotten to his feet and stood by the counter.

Kylie handed him several plates, then turned to look at Austin. "You can put Mercedes in her walker."

It was clear her mind was made up. She was leaving El Paso.

He'd missed his opportunity to change her mind back when they'd taken Lena in. Robert had talked him into coming over to see her one more time and say goodbye, thinking that might help the unsettled feelings he wrestled with.

He placed Mercedes in her walker, brushing a finger lightly over her rosy cheek. He felt like he couldn't breathe. How can someone so small, so fragile, have such a strong hold on his heart?

Kylie sat at the edge of the blanket. “This looks wonderful. Way better than I had planned. I dished up everyone’s plate. That seemed like the easiest way to do it.”

Austin sat down and crossed his legs while Kylie handed him a plate with canned cranberries, store-bought rolls, deli sliced turkey and green beans.

“A feast fit for a king,” said Robert. Robert’s cheerfulness sounded a little forced. He must be picking up on the tension between him and Kylie.

If he said he loved her, would she stay?

After saying grace, Austin took a bite of his roll and then scooped up some cranberries with a plastic spoon.

They ate, sharing small talk and laughing at the faces Mercedes made when Kylie fed her a bite of cranberries. Robert told a story about a Thanksgiving he’d spent in the jungles of Vietnam.

As they were finishing up the last bites of pie, Robert jumped to his feet and pointed at Mercedes’s stroller. “Why don’t I take the baby for a walk while you two clean up.”

“There’s not that much cleaning up to do.” Kylie seemed almost nervous.

Robert picked up Mercedes and sat her in the stroller. Mercedes kicked her legs. “I’m sure you two will find something that needs to be done.” He winked at Austin.

Robert wheeled Mercedes out the door with a backward glance and a smile. “I’ll be back in ten, fifteen minutes.”

Austin stood for a moment in stunned silence, wondering what on earth Robert expected him to do or say.

Kylie was leaving. He was pretty sure nothing he said would change her mind.

"We need to pick up the plates and take them out to the Dumpster." Kylie kneeled to get the remnants of the meal off the floor. "I don't have any garbage bags."

"I can carry them."

Kylie stacked the plates with the plastic cutlery on top. "This was a nice thing that you and Robert did." She stood up and handed him the plates. His hand wrapped around them, but she didn't let go. She looked at him, green eyes shining. "A nice thing you did for Mercedes and me."

His face flushed as the moment between them became electrified. "I'm going to miss you and that little squirt."

"So you keep saying." Her voice tinged with frustration.

"I want to say more."

"Then say it." Her eyes pierced right through him.

He pulled the plates from her hands and set them on a stack of boxes. He gazed at her for a long moment. He took her in his arms, resting his hand on the back of her head and drawing her close. His lips covered hers. Warmth spread through his whole body and burned a hole in his stomach.

She stepped closer to him as he deepened the kiss. He pulled back and kissed her forehead. He relished the sweet floral smell of her skin and the softness of her hair as it grazed his cheek. He held her close for a long moment.

Was this a goodbye kiss or…something else? He drew back to look her in the eyes. Her expression, the wide round eyes and slightly parted lips, suggested anticipation. She wanted him to say something, did she want to hear that he loved her? If he said it, would she stay or break his heart in two?

The realization of the pain she could cause him made him take a step back. He looked away, then picked up the plates. "I'll take these out." He headed toward the door without looking at her.

Austin stepped out into the cool winter day. An overcast sky suggested rain. He hurried toward the back of the apartment complex and flipped open the lid of the Dumpster.

He tossed the plates, feeling despair descend on him like a shroud. It was better this way. Kylie deserved more than he could give her. Mercedes deserved more.

"Hey." Kylie's voice sounded behind him and he turned to face her.

She rushed toward him, kissing him and then resting her hand on his cheek. Head tilted, eyes filled with light. "I love you. There, I said it first."

Her words were like a soothing balm. Words he had longed to hear his whole life. But this wasn't about what he needed. "Kylie, I wouldn't be a good father. I don't know how to be."

She kissed him again. "You've shown over and over that you love Mercedes. That you would die for her. Your actions show me that. Besides, I think fatherhood is a learn-as-you-go thing. At least, that's the way being a mom has been."

"You might be right." He traced along the edges of her face with his finger and nodded. He loved her too. Why couldn't he say it? "But, you're leaving."

Her expression clouded and she stepped away. "Is that it, then?" She turned.

"Kylie, no." He grabbed her arm just above the elbow

and twirled her around. He wasn't going to let her get away, not ever again. He drew her close and kissed her. "I love you too," he whispered in her ear. He kissed her cheek. "A thousand times. I love you too."

She wrapped her arms around his neck and gazed up at him. "Well, then. That settles it."

"Don't go. Stay here in El Paso."

She opened her mouth, ready to answer.

He kissed her again and spoke with his lips still very close to hers. "Stay here and marry me."

She pulled back to gaze into his eyes. She nodded slowly at first. "Yes, Austin. I'll stay, and I will marry you."

He brushed the back of his hand over her soft cheek. "We're going to have to come up with a better story to tell our daughter than me proposing to you by the Dumpster."

She laughed. "I like that story. And I like the idea that years from now we will tell it to *our* daughter."

"Yes, our daughter." He took her in his arms and held her close as the sense of joy and belonging he had searched for all his life flooded through him.

* * * * *

If you enjoyed THANKSGIVING PROTECTOR,
be sure to get the next book in the
TEXAS RANGER HOLIDAY *series—*
CHRISTMAS DOUBLE CROSS by Jodie Bailey.

And don't miss a book in the series:
THANKSGIVING PROTECTOR
by Sharon Dunn
CHRISTMAS DOUBLE CROSS
by Jodie Bailey
TEXAS CHRISTMAS DEFENDER
by Elizabeth Goddard

Dear Reader,

I hope you enjoyed the exciting and romantic journey that Kylie and Austin went on. One of my favorite scenes in the book is the final one where Kylie, Mercedes, Austin and Robert have a very nontraditional Thanksgiving. Many of us have an ideal picture in mind when we think of the Thanksgiving meal, a room filled with extended family and a table overflowing with homemade food, lots of laughter, cooking together and positive feelings. While this ideal is wonderful and should be celebrated, not everyone experiences holidays like that because of geographic separation, strained family relationships or financial struggle. Our Thanksgiving might seem to fall short of that beautiful picture.

Because of circumstances out of her control, Kylie is not able to give Mercedes the Thanksgiving she pictured for their first holiday together. Yet she is able to find something positive about the moment—that she and Mercedes are together. Wherever you are this holiday season, with family, alone or with friends, celebrating abundance or facing financial hardship, in good health or struggling with sickness, I encourage you to let go of that picture we all carry in our heads of the "ideal" holiday season. Instead, ask God to open your eyes and show you what you truly have to be thankful for. You won't be disappointed.

Sharon Dunn

COMING NEXT MONTH FROM
Love Inspired® Suspense

Available November 7, 2017

CHRISTMAS ON THE RUN
Mission: Rescue • by Shirlee McCoy

After a blackmailer threatens to kidnap Carly Rose Kelley's son unless she forges some antique jewelry, the widowed single mother turns to her son's uncle, Dallas Morgan—a man she's never met before—to keep her and her child safe.

LONE STAR CHRISTMAS RESCUE
Lone Star Justice • by Margaret Daley

On a mission in Big Bend Park, Texas Ranger Drake Jackson stumbles upon an unconscious woman and an infant boy. When it becomes clear Kay Rollins has amnesia and can't remember why someone would be stalking her, only Drake can protect them...and help uncover her past.

CHRISTMAS DOUBLE CROSS
Texas Ranger Holidays • by Jodie Bailey

Undercover Texas Ranger Colt Blackthorn's convinced Danielle Segovia is really a wanted criminal—until she's kidnapped right in front of him. Now Colt must keep her out of the clutches of the notorious drug cartel leader whose sister is a dead ringer for Danielle.

COWBOY CHRISTMAS GUARDIAN
Gold Country Cowboys • by Dana Mentink

Attacked and left for dead in the trunk of her car, Shelby Arroyo's rescued by cowboy Barrett Thorn. But someone is determined she won't live to uncover the secrets hidden in the mine she's been investigating.

UNDERCOVER HOLIDAY FIANCÉE
True North Heroes • by Maggie K. Black

Trent Henry broke Detective Chloe Brant's heart the last time they were undercover together, but now to bring down a designer-drug ring, she'll have to pose as his fiancée and take on three dangerous gangs.

SILENT NIGHT THREAT
by Michelle Karl

The week before Christmas, NASA astronaut Natasha Stark wakes up wounded on the side of the road with no memories. And her former fiancé, FBI agent Chris Barton, is determined to stop the men after her, especially when he discovers she has a daughter...and he may be the father.

LOOK FOR THESE AND OTHER LOVE INSPIRED BOOKS WHEREVER BOOKS ARE SOLD, INCLUDING MOST BOOKSTORES, SUPERMARKETS, DISCOUNT STORES AND DRUGSTORES.

SPECIAL EXCERPT FROM

Texas Ranger Colt Blackthorn has only one goal—catch Adriana Garcia, sister of a notorious crime boss and suspected killer of Colt's best friend. Finally, just before Christmas, he has his eyes on the target...or does he? A case of mistaken identity has put Danielle Segovia in harm's way, so it's up to Colt to make things right by keeping her safe.

Read on for a sneak preview of
Jodie Bailey's CHRISTMAS DOUBLE CROSS,
the exciting beginning of the new miniseries
TEXAS RANGER HOLIDAYS,
available November 2017 from Love Inspired Suspense!

"Ms. Segovia." Colt leaned forward, his dark eyes serious. "We have a problem."

Adrenaline jolted against Danielle's chest and throbbed in the bruise on her cheek. "Whatever you think I did, I didn't. I've never—"

"It's not you." Glancing down at his cell phone and flicking through a couple of screens, he said, "Do you know who Rio Garcia is?"

Danielle's head jerked back in shock. Rio Garcia was the leader of a notorious drug cartel. Everyone knew that name. He was known for his calculated cunning and his murderous rages, for his ability to slip away from the authorities even when they believed they had him cornered.

"I don't have any connection to him."

"But the men who tried to kidnap you tonight may."

Danielle's muscles went weak. If she wasn't already lying down, she'd melt to the floor. "Why?"

LISEXP1017

Colt didn't answer the question immediately. He stared at his cell phone for what felt like an eternity, then studied Danielle's face before passing the device to her without a word.

Hand trembling, Danielle took the phone.

At first glance, the woman staring back up at her could be her twin sister. They had the same hair, the same eyes, but the other woman had a small scar next to her ear. Still, the resemblance was enough to make her feel she'd fallen out of reality into a very bad horror movie. "Who is this?"

Colt studied her as though her reaction to what he was about to say was of vital importance. "Her name is Adriana Garcia."

Garcia. Heart pounding, Danielle stared at the woman. "She looks like me."

Holding out his hand, Colt took the phone and pocketed it. "She's Rio Garcia's sister. She's wanted by both sides of the law for multiple reasons, and both sides will do whatever it takes to get to her first."

"Why is he having to search for his own sister?" She couldn't fathom that sort of distance between siblings. "I don't understand."

"The most I can tell you is that she stole something from him, and he wants it back." He laid a hand on hers. "We had intel that suggested you were her, but as you know, that intel was bad. The problem is, we believe Rio Garcia received the same intel, and that those were his men who came after you."

Danielle shook her head. She wasn't hearing this. It couldn't be true.

Because if a killer like Rio Garcia believed she was the person he wanted, he would stop at nothing to drag her to him.